I0623554

VIETNAM BLACK

BRAD HARMER-BARNES

SEVERED PRESS
HOBART TASMANIA

VIETNAM BLACK

ISBN: 978-1-925711-62-2

For Charlie and Rey, as always.

PART ONE

GOING UP THE COUNTRY

CHAPTER ONE

Hanson's boots sunk into the muddy path leading to the base. Tracks and wheels had churned the soil into a cloying paste that no amount of sun could dry out. The occasional shout of welcome drifted across the air towards the squad, and it was nice to hear their voices, although most of the actual words were blotted out by the engines of jeeps or the rotor of a chopper. The weather in Vietnam was always hot, of course, but today seemed worse than usual. The weight of their packs and firearms felt twice as heavy after having been on the march for three days with zero engagements with the enemy. The most exciting thing to happen on this patrol had been a truck full of chickens driving past.

He smiled to himself. It really had been totally loaded down with the things. It wouldn't have surprised him if he'd seen a chicken driving the damn thing.

Why was he smiling? That wasn't funny.

Shit, he must be even more tired than he first thought.

Sergeant Reese stopped at the gate to quickly report that they'd made it back home without incident, then turned to face the squad. He started to speak, but his words were drowned out by the roar of a passing M113 armoured personnel carrier. Hanson tried to focus in on what he was saying, and managed to cotton on after a few words.

"…hit the showers, and grab some sleep. I'm going to talk to the Lieutenant, report to him that both Jack and Shit happened this time, and also see if I can't wrangle us some time off before we have to hit the trail again."

The sergeant stopped to wipe his forehead and grab a Marlboro from his front pocket. "With any luck this war will be over before we end up back out there again."

"Amen to that," muttered Private Turner, an African-American hunk of beef from Georgia. Hanson liked Turner. Hell, he liked all of the squad, even Private Bradley.

"Fall out, and get some rest." Sergeant Reese finished with a dismissive wave of his hand, already on his way to the Captain's office.

"You want me to come with you, sarge?" asked Hanson. He was hoping to make the leap to Sergeant once Reese's tour had finished, and that was only five short weeks away. He wanted to learn the ropes as much as possible before then.

"If you want to do that rather than grabbing some food and some sleep, then please be my guest. Hell, if I could, I'd get you to go along in my place, so as I could be the one getting some R&R."

"There isn't much R&R around here, sarge."

"Is there more than you get on the trail?"

"Yes, sir."

"Then shut the fuck up."

***

Lieutenant Nelson Talley was writing at his desk when they entered his tent. The base was relatively new, and the officers were all either sleeping in their offices, or working in their bedrooms, depending on how you chose to look at it. An electric fan was feebly pushing the hot air around the stale smelling room, and failing to make it feel any cooler. There was no respite from the heat in Vietnam. It was everywhere. You always sweated. You always stank. You were always thirsty.

Talley didn't even look up as Reese and Hanson entered and snapped salutes. He just continued checking off his paperwork. "Report."

"Echo Squad reporting back from patrol, sir. Sergeant Reese and Corporal Hanson commanding, sir."

"I said report."

"Absolutely nothing to report, sir. No contact with the enemy. Nothing unusual."

"You're in a war zone and you saw nothing unusual?" said Talley.

"Nobody here but us chickens, sir," said Hanson. He felt the sergeant next to him trying to suppress a smile.

Talley finished his paperwork at last and sat back in his chair, toying with his pen. He was young to be a commanding officer - barely in his thirties - but younger men than him were dying in the jungle. "You've got a New Guy. He's waiting outside."

Hanson remembered having seen a streak of piss standing outside Talley's tent, but hadn't taken much notice. It hadn't been long since they'd lost Private Jacobs. He'd been the FNG in the squad as well, but at least he'd hung around long enough for the rest of them to bother to learn his name.

Reese showed no emotion. "Yes, sir. Thank you, sir."

Talley nodded in acknowledgment, then leaned forward on his elbows. "You have new orders."

"Sir? Another patrol?"

"Not exactly. More of a search and rescue."

Reese and Hanson exchanged a glance. Talley continued.

"For some time now, we've been relying on information on Charlie's movement from a contact in the nearby village of Hai Trang. The doctor there, a Mister Bo Xuan, has been getting information to us through a radio he keeps in his hut. The information he can supply is limited, of course, but we take whatever we can get."

Hanson knew the man wasn't kidding. The North Vietnamese Army were one thing - they looked like military, and had the hardware to back it up. The Viet Cong, commonly referred to as "Victor Charlie" or - more often - just "Charlie", were something else. They were an insurgent force, with no uniform. That prostitute you'd picked up in Saigon or even that little old lady you'd met on patrol could be a Viet Cong agent, and you'd never know until it was too late. They could hide in plain sight, which made them terrifying. Some of the men said Charlie was worse, some said Nathaniel Victor (the NVA) was worse. Hanson didn't really care all that much. As far as he was concerned they were all bad news.

"You want us to go looking for this Xuan, sir?" Reese asked.

Talley nodded and threw a photo across the desk. Reese picked it up, and Hanson studied it over his shoulder. It showed a nondescript Vietnamese man in his late-forties.

"Please," continued Talley. "He's been silent for two weeks now, which is twice as long as he's ever gone before. It could be that his radio is broken, or that he simply has nothing to report, but - well - put simply, we have to fear the worst."

"We'll investigate, sir. When do we head out?" said Hanson.

Talley passed Hanson a folded up map. "Here's the location of Hai Trang. When's the soonest you can move out?"

Reese pulled the corner of his mouth back in a grimace. "We literally just got back, after three days on the road, sir."

"Get some rest and head out in the morning. Dismissed."

"Yes, sir."

Hanson followed Reese from the room. Talley was already back on his paperwork before the door swung shut behind them.

"So much for the R&R, sarge," Hanson muttered.

"Tell me about it. The boys are going to be pissed."

"You got that right."

They stepped outside of the tent and looked at the Private waiting for them. It was all Hanson could do not to suppress a laugh. The boy - for it would have been a stretch to call him a man - stood over six feet tall, but not a pound of him looked to be muscle. He'd heard the phrase "all skin and bones", of course, but never thought he'd see anyone embody it quite so literally. His blonde hair was almost transparent, and Hanson knew that he'd be lobster red inside of a week. The icing on the cake, however, was the feeble, almost invisible moustache the private was cultivating. If he didn't have any confidence in the US military's paperwork (and there was a joke for another time) he'd struggle to believe that the lad was over fifteen.

"All right, let's get this done," said the sergeant to the private. "I'm Sergeant Vincent Reese, and this is Corporal Michael Hanson. You're Private Falconer?"

"Yes, sir. It's pronounced "Faulk-ner", sir."

"Be that as it may, you can expect the squad to call you FNG for a while."

"Uh, if you say so, sir."

Reese swatted a flying bug away from his face. "I do say so. I'm not saying I agree with it or that it's the polite thing to do, I'm just telling you that it's what the rest of the squad *will* do. I make myself clear?"

"Yes, sir."

"You got all of your gear?"

"Yes, sir."

"All right. Let's head to the barracks. You can have Jacobs' old bunk."

"Uh, yes, sir. Thank you, sir."

"It's 'sarge', or 'Sergeant Reese'. Not 'sir'."

"Yes, sir-geant Reese."

Reese and Hanson headed straight to the barracks. Falconer grabbed his bags from the floor and jogged after them. Hanson shoved the doors open and the sound of the squad chatting and relaxing washed over him, accompanied by the sound of Hendrix over some tinny sparklers. No-one was sure where Turner had managed to acquire a record deck from, but nor did anyone complain. Turner was playing cards with Bradley - the other black guy in the squad. Turner was a large, yet easy-going man and Private Darterrius Bradley was pretty much his opposite in every conceivable way besides skin colour. Bradley was hyperactive, skinny and a troublemaker. Everyone knew he sold weed and acid around the base, but either the Captain and Lieutenants didn't care, or they were also customers of his, because nothing was ever done about it.

Private Walton, the squad's M60 machine gun operator, was crashed out asleep on his bunk already. That was exactly what Hanson was planning on doing as soon as he was able. Sleeping on the trail was always shitty. The chance of getting eight - hell, even five hours - straight sleep in a mattress was a prospect that excited him very much.

The last member of the squad, Private Liam Winters, was also on his bunk, but he wasn't asleep. He was propped up against the headboard, reading a heavily foxed sci-fi novel. Hanson was pretty sure he'd seen him read that one before, but if that was what relaxed the man, then that was what relaxed him. Winters was their radio operator, and his job could be a very stressful one; thankfully Winters seemed to be the most completely unshakable man in the whole war. Nothing - neither good nor bad - seemed to rattle him.

"Okay, listen up," said Reese. "This is your new guy. Be nice to him, I'm sure he'll be nice to you. FNG, that's your bed. Get some rest, we got orders that we're heading out again in the morning."

Sighs, groans and curses came from Bradley and Turner. Winters didn't seem concerned, and Walton just snored.

"There's good news, though, sarge," said Hanson.

"And what exactly is that, Corporal?"

"At least he didn't say 'first thing' in the morning. We can have a base breakfast before heading out."

"Superb. Snotty eggs, cold bacon and dirt coffee. I think I'm going to shoot my load in excitement. Anyway, I'm going to grab some food. You want to join me, corporal?"

"No thanks, sarge. I'm going to follow Walton's example, there. Some sleep sounds just about perfect to me, now."

"All right. Let's call it a day and go and grab breakfast at seven tomorrow morning."

"So much for the lie in, eh, sarge?"

"Get your ass to bed, Hanson."

Falconer had stowed his bags in his bed's foot locker. His bunk was the one next to Winters', and he tried to get a look at what the radio operator was reading. It had a strange, vibrant cover, depicting what looked like a spaceship of some kind. "Hey. I'm Alex. Alex Falconer. What's that you're reading?"

Winters seemed surprised that the FNG was talking to him. "Oh, uh…H.G. Wells' *The First Men in the Moon*. Have you read it?"

"No, I can't say I have. Is it about the moon landing?"

"Oh, no. Wells wrote it back in the nineteen-hundreds. I don't imagine it'll be especially accurate. We know a lot more about the moon now than we did back then."

"You read it before?"

"More times than I can count. I loved it when I was a kid, and now, well…it reminds me of being a kid."

Falconer smiled. "That makes sense, man."

Winters turned back to his book. It was obvious that he considered the conversation ended, and Falconer didn't know how to open it up again. He wasn't a hundred per cent certain he wanted to.

Hanson spoke to him from the bunk opposite Winters'. "Don't worry about Winters, FNG. He's our very own Robbie the Robot. A goddamned genius, but he can be difficult to talk to, if you follow me."

"Yes, Corporal."

"'Hanson is fine."

"Uh…okay, Hanson."

Hanson was already snoring, his rhythm slightly faster than that of Walton's in the corner. Feeling a little like a spare prick at an orgy, Falconer went over to where Bradley and Turner were playing cards. "Hey. I'm Falconer."

"I know, man, it's stitched onto your shirt," said Turner, throwing some more cigarettes into the pile in the middle of the table that made up the ante. "You a bird handler or something?"

"Uh, no. Like I say, it's pronounced 'Faulk-ner'."

Turner lit a cigarette, and looked at him skeptically. "It's pronounced FNG, unless you want us to call you Birdman instead?"

"Not particularly."

"Then shut the fuck up, FNG. We're trying to play here." Bradley, interrupted in a cocky, high-pitched gabble.

"Hey, I'm just trying to be friendly, guys."

"You want to be friendly, why don't you go spoon up with Walton, over there. Get the fuck out of here."

Falconer felt his blood rise, but knew better than to start a fight in the barracks on his first day - never mind his first fifteen minutes. He sucked up his grievances and sat back on his own bunk. After a few minutes, he got out a pad and a pen, and decided to write some letters home.

Hi Mom,

Just got here and have made some new friends already. I haven't had much chance to talk to the sarge yet, but the corporal (that's the second in command of our squad) seems very friendly. The guy in the bunk next to me seems nice, too. He was talking to me about a book he was reading.

We're heading out on a mission tomorrow, which is very exciting. I don't know what it is yet, but don't worry, I'm sure they won't send me anywhere too dangerous on my first day.

It's unbelievably hot here. Every room has a fan in it, but it doesn't actually cool you down at all. The only things that work are sitting in the shade with your shirt off, and drinking water. Don't worry, I won't drink any beer until I turn twenty-one, like I promised. Of course, that's only a couple of months away now.

I really miss you and little Marianne. Still, I'm hoping this will all be over before Christmas, and I can see the new year in back with you.

Love you with all my heart,
Alex

He knew he should write one to Audrey, too, but he didn't know what to say. There was every chance she had forgotten who he was already. He put his head down on his pillow, and tried not to think about what had happened to the last person to lay there.

CHAPTER TWO

Hanson gradually swam up from sleep, roused by the sound of Big Brother and The Holding Company on the turntable. That'd be Turner. The man was scared to do anything without music, regardless of what everyone else was up to. He grabbed his watch from the small bedside table and realised he'd been asleep for several hours, and it was now past half-seven in the evening. He swung his body upright and his feet onto the floor in one motion, rubbed at his stinging eyes, and looked around his squadmates. Not much had changed. Walton had woken up and was sat up in bed, smoking a cigarette - at least, Walton decided to assume it was just a cigarette, as he wasn't in the mood to deal with anything else.

Turner and Bradley were still playing cards. Winters had fallen asleep reading, and his paperback now lay where it had fallen on the floor. The FNG was laying down, but Hanson couldn't tell if he was asleep, or just trying to relax.

The air in there was stifling, the electric fans doing absolutely nothing to battle it. His stomach growled, and he decided that he was just hungry enough to face the base's food.

Outside of the shabby canvas and wood barracks it was even hotter. The atmosphere in the tent was close, but it wasn't in the direct sunlight. In there, you stewed. Out here, you baked. The base was as noisy as ever. Jeeps, M113 armoured personnel carriers and the constant hubbub of conversation continued even into the early evening. It would likely continue long into the night - if not all the way through. War never slept.

The canteen wasn't as busy as he would have expected so close to a conventional dinner time. There were fifteen, maybe twenty, people, all scattered about in small groups, chatting quietly. Sergeant Reese sat alone, rubbing his eyes, tiredly. He grabbed himself what was apparently some kind of chili and rice, and joined the sarge. "You look like you've gone ten rounds with Floyd Patterson."

"I feel like it. I've only got five more weeks, and I'm home. I was hoping I could stick it out with some nice quiet little bullshit jobs on the base. Now I'm marching deep into the jungle to talk to Charlie's informant. It wasn't exactly how I wanted to end my stay out here, you know?"

"I hear you."

"Five weeks and out."

"Yeah."

They fell quiet for a moment, stirring their food around on their plates. Hanson finally braved a bite. The meat wasn't too bad, but he didn't want to think about what it was. It tasted like beef, but he hadn't ever seen a cow near the base. "What are you going to do first thing when you get back?"

"Kiss my wife, and get a milkshake."

Hanson smiled. "The simple pleasures are the ones that you miss the most, right?"

"Fucking A."

"What do you make of the FNG?"

Reese shrugged. "Same as all the others were. He looks like someone tipped five pounds of straw into a uniform and glued a moustache to it, but we won't know until we see him in action. Could be he buys it within ten minutes of leaving the gate tomorrow. Could be that he's the greatest war hero this side of Iwo Jima. You just don't know, man."

"Right."

"Look, I've seen a lot of both types, and I'm telling you, you can't tell. There was one guy built like fucking Marciano, and he curled up into a ball and started crying as soon as he heard his first shot fired. It was a rifle going off maybe five hundred yards into the jungle, and it wasn't even aimed at him, but he just fucking broke."

Hanson swallowed some glutinous rice, which - to be fair to the chef - wasn't all that bad. "What happened to him in the end?"

"Pit trap."

"Sticks?"

"Yup. I can still hear him screaming sometime. He went back home, I don't know what happened after that."

Hanson nodded. Punji sticks were a favourite booby trap of the Viet Cong. They were simple in their design, and - while not likely to be immediately lethal - they were highly dangerous. He'd seen one guy fall into a pit trap where the sharpened bamboo stakes were dug into the sides of the pit, pointing downwards, meaning he couldn't free his leg without doing even more damage to himself. It had taken them over an hour to be able to dig him out; and that was the whole point of Charlie's traps. If they killed one man with a bullet, then the rest of the squad found them, and returned fire, and then marched on. If they wounded one man, then the entire squad was forced to slow down and take care of them. Rather than taking out one man, you effectively took out ten. It wasn't a new technique, historically speaking, but it was an effective one.

The sergeant took a sip of water from an almost clean mug. "Then there was a streak of piss, just like our FNG. First time we ran into any trouble, he just about went psycho."

"How do you mean?"

Sergeant Reese shrugged. "Just what I said, man. He went psycho. We were in a small village, like the one we're heading to tomorrow. When we got there, we found an arms and ammo dump, and suddenly Charlie pours out of nowhere, and we're in this absolute shit storm of a firefight. You know what it's like, though, I lose track of everyone."

"Sure."

"After the smoke has cleared and the dust has settled, there's that guy - Moore, his name was - and he's completely covered in blood...and not a drop of it was his. There's three dead Viet Cong at his feet, and he's completely covered in their blood."

"Shit."

"That weren't the weirdest part, man. The weirdest part was that his knife was clean, and his rifle was cold."

Hanson felt the hairs on his arms rise. "You mean, he…"

"Bare hands, man. Streak of piss just like our FNG."

"Fuck."

Reese pushed his tray to one side and lit a cigarette, offering the pack to Hanson, who took one gratefully. "Like I say, Corporal, you really can't tell. Big motherfucker - I mean bigger than Walton - cries like a baby, and a bunch of reeds like the FNG can rip men apart with his fingernails. War changes people, and you don't know how it's going to affect them until you see it with your own two eyes."

Hanson nodded, and rubbed his eyes. "Man, I'm still fucking tired."

"I want everyone to get an early night, okay? I'm not carrying any of your sorry asses if you decide to take a nap halfway through."

Hanson chuckled. "Anything you say, sarge."

***

Falconer awoke with a start and it took him a moment to remember where he was. The sun had just hit the horizon, and a strange orange light was just visible through and around the blinds pulled down over the plexiglass windows. He looked around the barracks, and the events of the previous day came back to him. Bradley and Turner were still playing cards for cigarettes. Winters - the radio guy who liked sci-fi - was asleep, and snoring gently. Corporal Hanson, Sergeant Reese and the large guy who had been asleep when he had first arrived were gone. He staggered to his feet. His whole body felt greasy and sticky with sweat, and he smelt like rancid cabbage soup. He grabbed a towel from his bag, and headed in search of the showers.

"Turn right, three tents down," said Bradley, not even looking up from his poker game.

"Thanks."

"My pleasure, FNG."

The base was quieter than when he'd first arrived, but definitely still alive and lived in. Conversations were muted now, engines less numerous and there were no choppers in earshot. He banged open the door to the showers, and saw that only one other person was in there - Walton, the large guy. Falconer had known that the guy was big, but hadn't been prepared for just how big. He had to be at least six foot four, and was muscular as hell - not overdeveloped like a bodybuilder, but built for strength. "Hey," he said, "you're the FNG, right?"

"Uh, yeah. Walton?"

"That's right." The man reached a hand over the chest-high partition that separated the showers, and Falconer shook it gratefully. It felt like the first time he'd been treated as human since arriving in Vietnam. "I'm the M60 operator. That means I do all the heavy lifting and all the heavy killing."

"Yeah, I tried firing one of those in basic training. They're pretty heavy, but also fun as hell to let rip with."

"You got that part right. I don't mind carrying the extra weight, to be honest. But, yeah. I'm Walton. Martin Walton."

"Alex Falconer."

Falconer stepped into the shower and yanked the chain. The water was only tepid, but to be honest, that was just perfect for the environment he was in. Who wanted to bathe in hot water when the atmosphere was as thick as soup anyway? You'd be walking in sweaty and walking out sweaty.

"Everyone's just going to call you FNG."

"Yeah, I'd noticed. At first I thought I'd pissed someone off."

Walton was scrubbing shampoo into his buzz cut. He'd squirted way too much into his hand and the top of his head was disappearing under a mountain of foam. "Nah, man. It's nothing personal it's just...promise me this won't upset you?"

Falconer was aware this was a blind promise, which was always a bum deal, but shrugged anyway, because that was what you were supposed to do in those situations. "Uh, sure. Lay it on me."

"They don't think it's worth learning your name, because they don't think you'll last here."

Falconer didn't quite know how to react. He froze for a couple of seconds before mumbling, "W-what?".

"It's nothing personal, and all of us here had to go through it. Until you've been here a couple of weeks - at least - people won't think it's worth learning your name."

Falconer felt cold. "Fuck. Man, how bad is it out there?"

Walton shrugged and rinsed his hair, eyes closed. "Bad enough most people don't last two weeks. That's just part of being the FNG."

"Right."

Walton stepped out of the shower, wrapped a towel around himself and picked up his bag. "See you back at the barracks?"

"Yeah. Sure. Uh, Walton?"

"Yeah?"

"What does FNG mean?"

Walton laughed. "Fucking New Guy. See you soon."

"Uh…yeah. See you soon."

Hanson and Reese got back to the barracks around nine. The corporal playfully clipped Turner around the ear. "Turner, how the fuck are you two still playing cards? You've been at it over six hours now. Don't you need to eat or sleep or go for a shit or something?"

"Hey, man," replied Turner in his laconic baritone. "When you're on a roll like this you don't walk away from the table for nothin'. Besides, what else am I going to do? Listen to Walton snore, or eat some fried rice bullshit in the motherfucking canteen? I think I'll just sit here if it's all the same to you."

"Man, you ain't on that much of a roll," said Bradley, his high pitched whine a strong contrast to his opponent's. "You're just glad you're not in my fucking pocket for once."

"Yeah, well, man, I've wound up in your pocket twice before and I ain't never going there again. It stinks of fucking weed for one thing."

Hanson raised a hand to interrupt them. "Hey, I'm not going to play mother, all right? Just make sure you get a good night's sleep. The sarge and I want everyone awake and alert tomorrow."

"Yes, sarge." They both replied.

Hanson and Reese collapsed into their bunks, and the poker game continued quietly, their voices falling to whispers.

"You ain't got shit," whispered Bradley. "I'll see your five and raise you three."

"Nice to see you putting your fucking money where your fucking mouth is," said Turner.

"Hey," said a whispered voice next to their table. They looked up to see Falconer standing next to them.

"Hey, yourself," said Turner. "We too noisy for you?"

The FNG looked kind of flustered, and confused. "Uh, no. Not that. Uh...I overheard what you were saying earlier and...you guys got any weed?"

Turner suppressed a laugh. "You come to the right place, new guy. Mr. Darterrius Bradley, here, is a man who knows how to get things."

"You got any now? I can't sleep and in the past it's helped me crash out."

Bradley watched him for a moment.

"I've got money," the FNG added, a little too keenly. It really did make him sound like a little high school kid trying to buy beer with a fake ID. "How much do you want?"

"How much do *you* want, new guy?" asked Bradley.

"I...I dunno, man. I've never bought any before, okay? I'm just fucking strung out, over here."

Turner and Bradley exchanged a glance and burst into muffled laughter, trying not to wake the rest of the squad.

"I say something funny?" Falconer asked, really starting to get pissed off now.

Bradley waved a hand, and reached into his shirt pocket. "Naw, man. You're good."

He handed him a rolled up joint. "Here you go."

"Thanks. How much do I..."

"You don't, new guy. Consider it a present."

"Really? Thanks."

"Don't mention it. Welcome to Vietnam."

***

When Falconer returned from smoking his joint, Turner and Bradley had called it a night. The canvas building was pitch black, the only noises the sounds of strange crickets and lizards, and Walton's snoring. Falconer half felt, half fumbled his way back to his bunk, the weed giving him a nice gentle high. He lay gently down on his mattress, and stretched out, his aching muscles finally starting to relax.

"Well done, new guy. You lasted one day," whispered Walton, in the bunk next to his.

"Thanks, man."

"Get some sleep. We're up in six hours. And believe me, that's the most we'll be getting until we find this gook informer."

"Is it really that bad out there?"

"No. It's worse."

CHAPTER THREE

At eight o'clock the following morning, all seven of them had gathered outside of the barracks. Walton was still yawning, and Falconer was still rubbing the sleep from his red, stinging eyes. Sergeant Reese stood in front of the rest of the squad, and gave them their briefing. "Okay, men, here's the deal. We - that is to say "the military of the United States of America" - have an informant working for us in the little village of Hai Trang, named Mister Bo Xuan. Mr. Xuan has been sending up information on Charlie's movement for the past year or so, but he seems to have suddenly gone quiet. Our job is to get to Hai Trang, check if Mister Xuan is okay; and if not, to find out what happened to him and report back. We're not anticipating running into any of the enemy, but - as most of you know - it's a jungle out there, so always be prepared."

An affirmative mumble came back at him. "Any questions?"

Walton raised his hand. "Sarge, how large is the village?"

Reese shrugged. "I don't have much information, but it can't be large at all. I'd be surprised if it was more than ten, maybe twelve, houses. Say…fifty to a hundred people."

"Gonna be hard to find. We got a map, at least?"

Reese smiled and threw a plastic wrapped bundle of paper. "Yes, we do; and you just volunteered to be map reader."

"Aw, fuck, sarge."

"Anyone else?"

"We got any air support?" asked Falconer.

"Negative. Hai Trang is in deep jungle cover. There's no way anything up in the air would be able to see it. Not with any degree of accuracy, at least. Again, though, I don't expect this to be a combat heavy mission. This is a search and investigate, not a seek and destroy. Is there anything else?"

The squad was quiet. "Okay, then. Move out."

Reese headed towards the main exit of the base, and Hanson fell in behind him, the rest of the squad behind. Once they were outside of the base, and heading towards the jungle, across a four hundred foot clearing that had been made as an improvised helipad for the base's three Hueys, Hanson jogged a little to stand next to the sergeant. "Reese, does any of this seem weird to you?"

"Hanson, everything about this place has seemed weird since I stepped off the bird. You'll have to be more specific."

Hanson lit a cigarette. "I mean, it seems pretty likely to me that this old man is dead already. What's the point in sending us at all?"

Reese laughed. "You've been here this long and you're still questioning orders? There's no point in questioning any of this shit, Hanson. Just do what you're told, keep your head down and go home at the end of your tour. You can do that, right?"

"Yes, sarge. Yes, I can."

Falconer's M16 felt heavy in his hands. He'd carried a bolt action rifle through most of basic training, and that had actually been a heavier weapon, but the rest of his gear and the oppressive heat had made tiredness creep in before he'd even reached the jungle. His eyes flicked to Walton, and he wondered how the man could carry his massive M60 in that heat.

Walton looked and him, and smiled. "I know what you're thinking, and don't worry: you just get used to it. You'll be running around in your gear in no-time."

Winters was bringing up the rear, looking intently around him, constantly scanning the area. Bradley dropped back and smiled at him. "Yo, Winters. How's it hanging?"

"It's hanging just fine."

Bradley chuckled, his high pitched voice was grating to almost everyone who heard it, but Winters never seemed affected. "You looking forward to getting back in the jungle? Maybe dropping a few gooks?"

Winters kept scanning the area, and shifted the radio on his back. "Not especially."

Bradley was the sort of person who rarely let silence fill a conversation, but he always found Winters incredibly hard to talk to. "So, man, where you from, anyway? You got anyone waiting for you at home?"

"Iowa. My Mum and Dad. You?"

"Brooklyn, man. Got my girl waiting for me back there. Man, she was a state when I left, crying her eyes out at the airport. Made me feel like she was convinced I was going to die already, you know what I'm saying?"

"Yeah. My Mum cried, too."

"What made you enlist, man?"

Winters shrugged. "The training. I want to be an electronics engineer, and this was better training than I'd get in college. It pays better, too."

"And you get to kill commies."

Winters shrugged. "What made you enlist?"

"The judge gave me a choice of that, or a stretch in the big house. Little scrawny guys like me don't fair too well in prison, you get me? But canny motherfuckers like me can fare pretty well in a war zone. I figured it'd be a better use of my abilities, plus - as you said - it pays better."

They had reached the edge of the clearing. This was where the jungle began.

Falconer felt his heart catch. He'd had the training. He'd seen the jungle from the plane, and from the chopper that had brought him to the base, and into Reese's squad. He rubbed at his feeble moustache, and had never felt so much like a little boy pretending to be a man as he did at that moment. Sweat ran down his back, and he fumbled a cigarette from the packet in his shirt pocket.

Hanson noted the young private's moment of stress and clapped him on the shoulder. "Don't worry. It gets easier each time."

Falconer nodded, not sure that he believed him.

Reese called back, "Turner, you're on point. Winters bring up the rear with Hanson."

Turner muttered something that was most likely a commentary on the sergeant's parentage, and stepped past him and into the jungle.

"It's strange, isn't it?" Walton whispered to Falconer. "It's like two different worlds smashed together. There's not even an inch of transition. It's just clearing…and then deep jungle. It's like we just cut the land with a knife."

Falconer didn't react, and just fell into step behind Turner. Reese fell in after him, and -one by one - the squad entered the jungle.

***

Within minutes, the humidity was so high it was like walking through a sauna. The plants around them seemed to have their own special way of trapping heat and moisture, reflecting it back at the intruders. Reese spoke gently to Falconer as they walked. "How's it going, new guy?"

"It's going good, sarge."

"You sure? Because if that's true, you're adapting to this a lot quicker than any sane man does."

Falconer smirked. "I'm fine, sarge."

The conversation paused momentarily as they staggered across a particularly dense knot of roots and vines on the jungle floor. Once they were past, Reese spoke up again. "So, who's Audrey?"

"What?"

"You've got Audrey written on your helmet. She your girl back home? Your daughter? Your sister?"

"My girl back home. Kinda."

"How do you mean 'kinda'?"

"She…doesn't really know that she's my girl."

"Say what?"

Falconer was blushing bright red. "We went to high school together. She's smart and pretty, and just really cool. It's just I…never got the courage to ask her out, because I didn't think she could be interested in a scrawny little guy like me."

"The hell she wouldn't, new guy. You mean you couldn't scrape up the nerve in - what - two, three years of knowing the girl?"

Falconer shrugged. "I figured I stood a better chance if I was an army vet, you know. I'd be stronger, tougher, braver. So, I signed up to her impress her, and when I go back home, I'm gonna ask her out."

Reese was speechless for a second. "You mean to tell me that you weren't brave enough to ask a girl to go to the drive-in with you, so instead you decided to fly halfway around the world to spend twelve months being eaten by mosquitoes and shot at by gooks, just so you can impress her?"

"Well, sarge, when you say it like that it sounds silly."

"You're fucking insane, new guy, you know that?"

Up at the head of the line, Turner stopped suddenly and threw up his palm behind him, telling the rest of the squad to halt. Everyone froze, and a couple of whispered curse words wafted up the line. Hanson moved up the line and squatted down next to Turner, scanning the jungle for any sign of a contact. "What is it?" he asked.

"Tripwire," replied Turner, pointing to a thin line of woven rope stretched across the pathway. Hanson followed it along its length. One end was tied around a short stake driven into the ground just off the edge of the path, and the other led across the path, into the jungle, and around the other side of a large tree.

Hanson wiped sweat from his forehead. "Good spot, Turner. You wait here, I'm going to go and show the FNG what you've found, and I'll disarm it."

"Roger that."

Hanson backed down the line, to Reese and Falconer. "Trap. Won't be a second, sarge. FNG, you come with me."

Falconer exchanged a quick glance with Reese, and then followed Hanson into the jungle. As they stepped around the side of a tree, Falconer felt his arm hairs rise. "What the fuck is that?"

On the blindside of the tree stood a five foot high lattice work of bamboo and branches, looking for all the world like a giant waffle. Peppered all around it were wicked looking, sharpened bamboo stakes. The tripwire went to its foot, and disappeared into a knot of string and pegs.

"That's what would have slammed into Turner if he hadn't have been awake enough to spot the tripwire, new guy. That's why we all tried to get a good night's sleep last night. One misstep and we're a good man down, you got me?"

Falconer had stepped closer to the booby trap and was studying it, morbid curiosity getting the better of him. "What's this stuff on the spikes?"

"Gook shit."

"What?"

"They do it with their pit traps, too. They smear their shit all over the spikes, so that if you get impaled, you also end up with a fucking nasty blood infection. It's never about killing you; remember that. It's about how bad they can wound you, and scare the shit out of the rest of the team."

"Jesus Christ."

Hanson examined the knot of pegs and string at the base of the tree for a moment, before cutting through a length of the rope with his knife. "Clear." He called back to the trail, and stood back up. "You ready, new guy?"

"Yeah. I…thanks for showing me, Hanson."

"Anytime."

They marched on - Turner leading, Walton navigating - for another two hours, deep into the jungle, before Reese finally called a halt. The noises of insects, birds and other strange creatures made Falconer feel as though he were on some alien world, rather than the jungle of East Asia. He sunk down onto a fallen log and lit a cigarette. Walton sat next to him and lit one of his own. "How are you finding your first day so far?"

"Man, it's literally nothing like I expected."

"At least you're honest. The worst are the guys…like Bradley was, over there…who pretend like nothing about it is rattling them. Bradley talks a good fight, but he was skittish as a cranked up gopher the first month he was here. Then he became the lovable, relaxed, easy going private we all know and love."

Falconer laughed, tapping his ash on the floor. "I don't think anyone here likes me."

"Ah, that's just part of settling in. I like you fine, and I can tell the sarge and Corporal Hanson do. The others are a bit harder to read, but even if they don't like you, they don't actively hate you either."

"Thanks, man."

"You'll be fine."

"I appreciate it, man. I just wanna do my thing here and then I'll…what is it?"

Walton's eyes had gone wide, and was staring at a point directly behind Falconer. "Don't move."

Falconer suspected the man was winding him up, but still didn't move. "What is it? You fucking with me, man?"

"Ssssh."

Falconer's voice fell to a whisper, and he froze completely still. "What the fuck is it, man?"

"Don't move."

"I ain't fucking moving, man! Just tell me what the fuck it is and I'll relax!"

Turner's voice came from somewhere to his left, but he daren't turn his head. "Aw, man, that's a big one."

"The fuck are you guys talking about? I swear, man, if you two are just fucking with me, here…"

Quick as a flash, Walton reached and grabbed something on his back. When he brought his hand back where Falconer could see it, he felt his gorge rise. "What the fucking fuck is that, man?" he screamed.

In Walton's hand, gripped between his thumb and first two fingers, was what looked like a seven inch long reddish brown snake, but with strange, yellow-orange legs covering its length. Walton had it gripped just behind its head, and a monstrous pair of mandibles gnashed and snapped, trying to grab a hold of the large man. "Centipede, man. You've never seen one of these things back home? I mean, they're nowhere near this big, nor this aggressive, so…"

"How the fuck did that get on my back?"

The rest of the squad, amused by Falconer's screams was watching and chuckling. Turner stooped down for a closer look. "That is a big boy. As for how it got on you…hell, any way that it wanted to. It might have crawled up when you sat on the log. It might have dropped on you from a tree a few hundred yards back and we only just spotted it."

"Jesus. Is it poisonous?"

Walton shrugged, watching the vicious centipede thrash around. The length of its body had wrapped around his wrist and he had to shake it to shuck it off. "You'll notice you've been bit, and it's supposed to be painful as shit - about as bad as getting shot - but it won't kill you. Unless you're allergic."

"How do you know if you're allergic?"

"You die when one of them bites you."

"You're kidding me?"

Walton laughed, and spun around, pitching the centipede up high and deep into the jungle. Falconer heard it clatter through the leaves and bracken, and Walton turned back with a smile. "Welcome to Vietnam."

CHAPTER FOUR

The hike continued, and the deeper they went into the jungle, the more oppressive the heat became. The humidity was the worst, as all the moisture was trapped by the plant life, making it feel as though the entire country was turned into one giant sauna. They had been working their way downhill and, in an instant, the trees gave way to a well trodden path, the widest they'd seen in a long time, forty feet across. In one direction it curved around a shallow bend, and in the other it simply stretched off into the distance.

"Huh. Must be an old trail," muttered Turner.

"Not so old," said Hanson. "These are tracked vehicle marks. Someone has been coming through here, and likely since it last rained."

"NVA?" asked Falconer.

"I don't think so. Too close to our base for them to be moving heavy vehicles through without us being aware of it. I don't think that any of the farmers round here have tractors, so I think it's either us or the ARVN using it for supply runs."

"You don't think it could be tanks?"

"Maybe, but, unlikely. Of course, I could be completely wrong and we're looking at an NVA tank battalion. Keep 'em peeled."

Falconer scanned up and down the path that continued long into the distance in either direction. Bradley waved a hand, dismissively. "Whoever it is is long gone by now. Let's get moving. Sooner we check out this missing gook the sooner we can get back to the poker table."

"Fucking amen, man," chuckled Turner.

Reese threw a hand up, calling for quiet, and the squad caught on fast. "Walton, get on the map and figure out which way is the best for us to head. I also want to know why this trail took us by surprise. Two men in each direction, keeping watch, the rest of us back into cover. Turner, I want you in cover with the grenade launcher."

Bradley and Falconer took one direction, Winters and Hanson the other. They stood boldly, rather than hunkering down on the ground. They wanted to send a visual message of confidence and look like they were working a police action, rather than just a bunch of Yanks lost in the jungle. Looks counted for a lot.

Hanson could hear Walton and Reese arguing over the map, whispered curse words floating in the humid air. He smirked at Winters. "How come you never volunteer to be map reader? Human computer like you ought to be real good at it."

"I did a few times in my last squad. They didn't like how I did it."

"What? How do you mean?"

Winters shrugged. "I made them swim a lake rather than go around it. It saved a lot of time, but as they got out the other side they saw the crocodiles."

Hanson laughed out loud, getting a glare from Reese. "Yeah, that makes sense."

"They're Siamese Crocodiles. They are very unlikely to attack humans. I made a calculated risk."

"Winters, with the utmost respect, I think we'll let someone else handle the map reading while I'm Corporal."

Winters shrugged. "Suits me."

Falconer tapped Bradley on the arm, and the hyperactive Bradley flinched away. "The fuck you doing that for man? The fuck is up with you, new guy?"

"Shut up. You hear that?"

Bradley cocked his head. "Man, I can't hear shit over the birds and bugs round here. Same as always, man."

"Listen. It sounds like an engine."

Bradley listened harder. He *could* hear something in the distance. "Yeah, man. I think you're right." He turned and called over to the other two. "Yo, the FNG thinks he hears something. You guys hear anything?"

"Negative," called back Hanson.

"It's coming from this direction," shouted Falconer.

Winters and Hanson jogged over to them so that they could face the oncoming vehicle together. They stood easy but confident. Hanson slung his rifle, and folded his arms. The three privates stood with M16 rifles lowered, but still held in both hands, ready to snap up in under a second.

The engine noise was getting louder, and they could now also hear the distinctive crank and whistle of a tracked vehicle. "It's got to be right around the bend," whispered Falconer.

"FNG, man, shut the fuck up," snapped Bradley.

"Both of you, ease down," said Hanson. "Stand ready."

Hanson's glance flickered to Reese, Turner and Walton in the undergrowth. He could only see them because he knew where to look. If this did turn out to be an enemy vehicle, those three would be invisible, and able to return some pretty heavy covering fire. Walton had the large M60 machine gun, and Turner had the M79 grenade launcher. Neither were going to be overly effective against an armoured fighting vehicle, but they should be able to provide cover while the four of them ran back into the jungle.

At last, the vehicle came around the bend.

It was an olive green, boxy looking thing; definitely built for economy and practicality rather than style or excess. Hanson recognised right away that it was an M113 armoured personnel carrier, meaning it was either part of the US military, or with their South Vietnamese allies, the ARVN. As it drew closer, the driver obviously spotted them and hit his brakes, before picking up again, at a lower speed this time. One of the men riding up top with the turret raised an arm in salutation, and Hanson returned the gesture. The cranking, whistling noise of the engine slowed down in pace with the M113, and it finally ground to a halt a few yards away from the group.

Hanson waved to Turner, Reese and Walton, who stepped out of the jungle and onto the path. The M113 stood about eight feet tall, so they had to look up to see the two men sat on the top. One was the driver, hunkered down in a recess, and the other was the gunner, sat slightly higher, behind an armoured plate which housed the .50 caliber machine gun. A crewman leapt down, and walked over to them.

Now they were closer, they could see that they were indeed ARVN - South Vietnamese. The crewman, who they now saw must be the commander of the squad inside, waved to them informally, and smiled. "Howdy, soldiers!"

Reese smiled back and extended his hand, which the small man accepted, and gave his name and their unit. "What are you boys doing around here?"

The man, who had given his name as Trieu Loi, shrugged. "We are just on patrol. Keeping an eye out for Viet Cong. Making sure that you men with your big guns don't run into any unnecessary trouble. You had any?"

Reese shrugged and lit a cigarette, then offered the pack to Trieu Loi. "Nothing much. We found a punji stick trap earlier, back that a ways. No hard contact, though. Yourself?"

Loi gratefully accepted a cigarette and a light. "We've seen signs of movement, but no hard contact. Trails messed with. Some pit traps. We think the Viet Cong are using tunnels around here."

"Tunnels? What kind of tunnels?"

"Some small dugouts for ambush. Some larger supply networks. Some of the tunnels the Viet Cong dig are insane, you follow, Yankee? Some run for miles underground, and can be full of men, food and bullets. You could walk right past and never know they were there."

"I had heard stories, yeah. You think they're round here?"

Loi hesitated, then nodded. "We've seen signs."

Reese could tell the man was on edge and walked with him away from the group. The rest of his squad made some small talk with the crew of the APC; at least as much as they were able to. Winters and Hanson spoke some Vietnamese, but they were far from fluent. They could probably order a beer and some noodles, but they weren't in any danger of getting a job on South Vietnamese television. When they were ten yards or so away, Reese stopped and addressed the man again. "Okay, tell me what you've seen."

"Some small things, like I already say. Signs of movement. Empty ration packets. The Viet Cong are good, but sometimes they make mistakes."

Reese studied him, and knew the man was hiding something. "Come on, man. There's a pack of smokes in it for you if you tell me what you know. And I know. And you know that I know that you know. So let's cut to the chase."

"Smokes? Camels?"

"I got Marlboro, man. Take it or leave it."

Loi shrugged, and gestured off handedly back the way they had come. "Back that way, we passed a Bulldog."

Reese exhaled a cloud of smoke. The Bulldogs were a light tank that the ARVN used, mostly thanks to the influence and support of the US forces. "Right…"

"It was blown up. Like it had exploded, ripped to shreds."

"So? The VC around here have RPG7s, right? A well placed rocket propelled grenade would make short work of a light tank like the Bulldog. No offence to your great nation, but your tanks aren't exactly built to the standard of the Patton we got."

"That's the strangest thing, Yankee. The armour of the tank was punched in in several places, but there was no sign of burning. No sign of heat. It was as though a large spear had been jabbed into and through it, again and again."

This did give Reese a reason to pause. What non-explosive could make a dent on a tank, even a lightweight piece of crap like the ARVN had? "That'd have to be some spear, Loi, and thrown by one hell of a big guy."

"Exactly, Sergeant. That's what I'm trying to tell you. It was very strange. No heat. No fire. No scorching. No smoke damage. Just a penetrated tank."

"What about the crew?"

"Gone."

"Gone dead, or gone walked away?"

Loi flicked his finished cigarette away. "Does it matter?"

"It sure does. Did you see bodies?"

"No, no bodies. But there was…something."

Reese was beginning to tire of this man's irritating way of dodging questions and phrasing evasive answers. "Bullshit, Loi. What did you see?"

"Dog tags on the seats and floor. A cap. Some boots. Photos left stuck to the insides of the tank."

"Personal effects."

"Yeah. If they walked away, why did they leave that stuff behind? If they're dead…where have their bodies gone?"

"Yeah, sounds a regular Marie Celeste all right."

"What?"

"Nothing. So you found this tank down the road…"

"About three miles, give or take."

"…about three miles down the road. Its armour has been penetrated in several places, by something non-exothermic." He knew the man wouldn't know the word 'exothermic' and got a sadistic little kick out of his momentary confusion. "The crew are all either dead and missing, or gone AWOL leaving all their shit behind. That about the long and short of it?"

"Yeah, that about the long and short of it in a nutshell. You got those smokes?"

"Loi, it's a good ghost story, and a good story is always worth a pack of smokes." He slapped a pack into the man's hand. "Now, tell me this…what do you think happened to the missing crew?"

The man shrugged. "I think they're dead. Either Viet Cong take the bodies into the woods, or the bugs and lizards eat them. Bugs here can strip a dead goat to bones in a week. To nothing in a month. Something hit the tank - I don't know what, but it took them all out, and the bugs took the rest."

"Yeah, we found one of your bugs earlier today. You have some truly beautiful wildlife in this country, you know that?"

"Between the tigers, the crocodiles and the spiders you don't got to worry about the Viet Cong."

"You got that right. You got some big ass spiders here."

"Most of them will keep out of your way. The black ones are the worst. They'll attack anything, and if they bite…you need a doctor."

"The black ones are no good, huh?"

Loi nodded, and ripped open his newly won packet of cigarettes, passing one to Reese. "Same goes for the scorpions. The Black Forest Scorpion will hurt bad. Maybe not kill you, but avoid all the same."

"Black ones are to be avoided in general. I got you. Same go for the snakes, yeah?"

"Right."

"Thanks, Loi. Look, we're headed for the village of Hai Trang. You heard of it?"

"Yeah, sure. I know it. Small farming village. Probably only twenty, maybe thirty people in the whole village, including women and children."

"Only twenty or thirty people? Man, that's even smaller than I thought. What they got there?"

Loi lit his cigarette and shrugged. "Nothing much. What's the Yankee interest?"

"That's classified, Loi. How far is it from here?"

"On foot? Through the jungle? A fair way. I hope you brought tents with you."

"How far, Loi?"

"Two days march, maybe? It's a way. You guys got food and water?"

"Yeah, we got supplies, thanks. And we can always snack on Vietnam Black Tarantulas and Snakes if we get hungry."

"You get hungry, I don't think you should eat them."

"Relax, Loi, I was kidding." He clapped him on the shoulder and began guiding him back towards the M113. "It's been a pleasure talking to you, Loi. Maybe when this is all over, I'll come back to the Vietnam, and we'll go out for dinner."

Loi nodded, once again failing to notice the sarcasm. "That would be wonderful."

A few seconds later, the armoured personnel carrier and Loi had trundled up the road away from them, and off into the distance.

"You learn anything useful, sarge?" Falconer asked. "Any inside info?"

"Man, shut the fuck up," said Bradley. "If the sarge learnt anything, he'll tell you if you need to know, you got me?"

"Sorry, I just…"

"Just what, man?"

Reese rested a hand on Bradley's shoulder. "Ease down. No, they got nothing to report. They hit a brewed up tank down the road, but it's in the other direction from where we're headed. Walton, I want you to get on that map and plan out a route for us. Apparently we're going to be stopping at least one, maybe two nights, before we hit Hai Trang. See if you can pace us out, okay?"

"Roger that, sarge," said the big man. "I"m not just a pretty face."

"Take five while Walton works that out, guys. Hanson, you're on point when we move out. Falconer, you're with me, and if I hear one inane question out of you, you're sharing a sleeping bag with Bradley. I make myself clear?"

Bradley muttered under his breath, and Falconer nodded.

He was gradually making sense of this strange world he had entered, and he was learning that he was the fucking new guy.

CHAPTER FIVE

The first night in the jungle passed without incident for most of the squad. Falconer was constantly woken by the strange noises around him. He was ready for the wind and the insects and the occasional drum of water from the trees hitting his poncho. He wasn't used to the wildlife being constantly awake through the whole night, and it kept him on edge. He wasn't scared of the animals themselves, but he was worried that the screech of a monkey, bat or some weird lizard, would mask the sound of an enemy advancing on the camp through the night.

Reese made sure that there was always two of them on watch, of course, but this did nothing to ease Falconer's broken sleep. Visions of the reddish brown centipede from that morning kept coming back to him, and sometimes, as he was just nodding off, he would suddenly flinch awake, convinced that he'd felt something slithering down his collar, or running across his face.

The sun came up at just before 5:30 in the morning, and the groans and cursing from the squad told him that he wasn't the only one who had slept badly.

"Okay, men, round 'em up," shouted Hanson, rubbing the sleep from his eyes. "Walton, you got our itinerary planned for today?"

"Yes, I have!" Walton shouted back, pointing a finger into the jungle. "That way for fucking miles!"

The whole squad laughed, and even Sergeant Reese smiled. "Just what we need. A long day's march in full gear, into enemy territory, to look for someone who might not even be there."

"That's Vietnam, baby!" Bradley shouted back, to a chorus of grumbled agreement.

Hanson and Walton took point, the rest of the squad following behind, with Winters in the rear.

"So," asked Hanson. "What do you make of the New Guy?"

Walton shrugged and lit a cigar. "I think he's okay. I think everyone is being too hard on the poor guy, the sergeant included. That's the way it is, though, ain't it?"

"Yeah. That's the way it is."

"I think he'll do okay. He's ready to learn, and I don't think he wants to be the one to let the squad down. That'll count for a lot."

"You remember when I was new guy, right?" Hanson asked, bending a branch back from the thin, barely visible path in front of him.

"Yes, I do."

"What did you think of me? Honestly now."

"I thought you were going to be okay."

"Seriously?"

"Seriously. Some guys I get a bad feeling with. With you - and with Falconer - I got a good feeling. I think you'll both be flying home at the end of this."

"We all fly home," said Hanson. "Just that some of us do it in a box."

Walton shook his head. "Not everyone. Sometimes they can't find enough to make it worth the flight."

Hanson nodded in assent. "Yeah, I remember."

Walton stopped suddenly, throwing up his hand behind him to indicate that everyone else in the squad should freeze, too. They all did so, even Reese and Hanson.

Hanson scanned the area, trying to see what it was that the gunner had seen. He couldn't see any booby traps in the path in front of them. There didn't seem to be anything in the trees, either. "What is it, Walton?" he whispered. "Charlie?"

"I'm not sure," the large man whispered back. "Over there. You see it?"

Hanson followed to where Walton was pointing. About thirty metres away, in the undergrowth, he could make out a pale-yellow, obviously man-made, object. It was a conical hat, of the type that the locals called a "nón lá". Now that he could see the top of the hat, he could just about make out some black cloth behind it, which could be the shirt or pants of the wearer.

"It could be Charlie. Could be a farmer. Could be some discarded clothes." Hanson couldn't tell from where he was. "We're gonna have to find out, though. We can't risk just strolling past him if the son of a bitch has a gun. Or grenades."

Reese had slowly crept up the line. "What's going on? Tripwire?"

Walton shook his head and pointed again. "Could be Charlie."

Reese spotted the hat quickly. "Shit. Okay, we're going to have to go check. Could just be a farmer, got himself some moonshine out here and passed out."

"Here's hoping, sarge."

Reese nodded. "Hanson, you take the new guy and go check it out."

"Well, *thank you*, sarge. Come on, new guy."

Falconer followed the corporal as they broke away from the squad in a right angle, hoping to approach the man from the side. Hanson led the way, treading carefully, so as not to crack any branches or knock over any loose stones that could alert the wearer of the hat to their presence. Every few steps, he stopped to look around.

"What are you looking for?" Falconer asked, his voice barely above a breath.

"If it is Charlie, then there won't be just the one of them."

He could see that this rattled Falconer. The FNG paled and joined in looking around. Well, if it had spooked him, that was a good thing. They weren't in the place to sugar coat the facts and ease him in gently any more. It was a combat zone, and they may well be engaged with the enemy.

They were now parallel with the mystery man. Hanson threw a glance over in the squad's direction to see if they had noticed anything that he and Falconer would have been unable to. Reese shook his head slowly. Winters was aiming his M16 at the man, and Walton was readying his large M60.

Hanson readied his own rifle, and slowly began advancing towards the man. "You still keeping an eye out, new guy?"

"Both fucking eyes wide fucking open."

"Good man."

His adrenaline was now running so high that it felt as though everything around him was thrown in sharp focus. His five senses were going crazy with soaking up all the information they could. He could hear the rustle of the leaves under his boots, feel the wind whistling across his skin. The tiny folds and dents on the man's rice hat was suddenly crystal clear; he felt as though he could actually see the molecules of the air around it.

They were only about ten feet from the man, now. There was no sign of movement.

Six feet. The undergrowth crunched a little, and Falconer spun around to face it, rifle raised. Nothing else moved. He kept his gaze focused on it, and relaxed a little as a small rodent - some sort of possum-type creature - trotted past.

Hanson had reached the man, and the man was long dead.

He could tell just by smelling.

The man lay on his back, looking straight up at the sky. With the barrel of his gun, Hanson gently lifted the brim of his nón lá. The face beneath it belonged to a man in his late thirties, maybe early forties, but the skin was pulled tight and waxy, accentuating the skull beneath. An AK-47 assault rifle rested on the ground next to him, but there was no sign of any other troops.

Hanson looked over to the squad and waved that it was okay for them to come over. He and Falconer kept a watch on them as they approached, still aware that the cadaver itself could be bait for some convoluted trap or ambush.

When they reached them, Reese and Walton stood by the dead man while the rest of the squad watched the trees around them. Reese lit a cigarette and studied the cadaver. "He looks desiccated. Must've been out here a while."

"Yeah. Rifle's right there."

Reese shrugged. "One less Charlie for us to worry about."

"Fewer," interrupted Winters.

Hanson prodded the body with the barrel of his rifle. "There's something weird about this, but I can't work out what."

"You wanna do an autopsy on the guy?"

Hanson pressed the barrel to the man's stomach. The skin stretched like rubber, then gave. He stumbled as the barrel sank a couple of inches into the body. "Shit!"

"You're gonna have to clean that, you know?"

Hanson felt his arm hairs rise as it dawned on him what was wrong with the dead man. He dropped quickly to his knees and ripped open the man's shirt. His skin was drawn tight against his chest and his ribs were clearly visible. There was something very strange about the man's stomach. There was a small hole where Hanson's rifle had penetrated the rubbery skin, but inside was just a dark nothingness. "Sarge?"

"What is it, Hanson?"

"His insides. All his organs are gone."

"The fuck are you talking about?"

"Just what I'm telling you, man. He's been gutted clean."

Reese dropped down next to the dead body and peered at its stomach. "So they are. Looks like something just...yeah, someone just gutted him like a fish."

"Charlie do this, you think?" asked Hanson. "Maybe this guy was a traitor, and this is some kind of gangland killing thing?"

Reese grabbed the dead man's AK-47 and pulled the clip out. "Half-empty. If this was Charlie they'd have taken the gun; or at least the ammo. If this was an execution, why would he have had his gun at all?"

Hanson stood back up. "Winters, Falconer, Bradley. Check those trees for any sign of bullet holes."

They murmured acknowledgement and walked off in the direction he had gestured.

"We're wasting too much time here, man," Sergeant Reese grumbled. "Who gives a shit about a dead gook. We oughta be in Hai Trang by now. Yo, Walton, when we gonna reach the village?"

"Tomorrow morning, sarge, if we keep to schedule."

"Corporal Hanson wants to play Sherlock Holmes with this guy a little longer. You boys don't mind, do you?"

"Hell no, sarge."

Bradley shouted back to them from a nearby tree. "Sarge! This one's full of rounds. Could be an AK."

"This one too!" Falconer yelled from another tree, about ten metres away.

"So this guy was in a firefight, and all the rest of them got away," said Sergeant Reese. "You happy now?"

Hanson pulled back the man's shirt and showed the sergeant a large puncture wound in the man's side, just below the rib cage. "That doesn't look like a bullet wound to me."

"Bayonet?"

"Nuh-uh. Not unless it's a round bayonet, four inches wide."

Walton, apparently confident that there were no Viet Cong in the trees or surrounding scrubland waiting to launch an ambush, had joined them and pointed at the wound with his cigar. "There's hardly any blood."

"So?" Reese asked. "And why aren't you on watch, soldier?"

Walton ignored the question. "I'm just saying that if that's the wound that killed him, then this whole area - not to mention his pants - should be red with blood. Something else, though: if someone stood here and pulled all his organs out, why's there no blood? He's just been...he's just been left here."

Hanson felt his arm hairs rise, and one look told him that Walton and Reese felt it, too. There was a sense that something very strange - maybe paranormal - had happened here, and the lack of an immediately rational explanation was more than they could cope with.

"Turn him over," said Hanson. "I want to get to the bottom of this."

Reese reached out a hand and stopped him. "No fucking way. I've heard of Charlie doing this before. There's every chance that there's a goddamn claymore under this guy, and as soon as you turn him over we all go bang. All we've got here is a dead gook. I don't know if he was VC or if he was just in the wrong place at the wrong time. Hell, he could have just had a heart attack here, and then God knows what animals and bugs out here ate what they could get at."

"That doesn't explain that puncture wound," muttered Hanson.

"I say we're out of here. We're leaving him and that's that."

Walton was now crouched down, poking the man's stomach. "He's fucking hollow, man. I ain't never seen anything like it."

Reese grabbed hold of the big man's arm and dragged him to his feet. "Didn't you hear what I fucking said? This guy could be rigged to blow, and you're prodding and poking the son of a bitch? And why the hell aren't you on watch? Get on fucking point, Private, and get us to Hai Trang."

"Yes, sarge," said Walton, contritely. He glanced at the map for a nanosecond, pointed back out of the clearing and started walking. "This way."

Reese and Hanson stood by the dead man as the rest of the squad filed by, Bradley bringing up the rear. When they had all passed by, Reese spoke to Hanson. "This is weird, right?"

"It's weird. Weirdest damn thing I've seen in Vietnam."

"That's a hell of a statement, Corporal."

"Yes, it is."

Reese flung his cigarette to the floor, and ground it out with his boot. "This guy had to be Charlie. He's got the black shirt, black pants and a fucking AK. So, where are the rest of them?"

Hanson shouldered his rifle and started following the rest of the squad. "Not here. They must've run."

Reese shivered. "This is fucked up."

Hanson slowed down, and gestured to the ground about five feet away. "You want another mystery?"

Reese looked to where he was pointing.

A severed arm, holding an AK-47 by the handle, the torn sleeve around the shoulder black with dried blood, lay in the grass.

Hanson stepped over and looked closer. "It's bled out, same as the guy back there. It's just skin and bone...maybe some fat. Barely any blood."

"Where the hell is the rest of him?" asked Reese.

Hanson prised the assault rifle from the cold, stiff fingers and pulled out the magazine. "Empty."

"What?"

Hanson threw it back to the jungle floor. "This guy emptied his magazine at somebody, and they still managed to get close enough to hack his arm off."

Reese grabbed his arm. "Come on, man. We gotta keep up with the squad."

Hanson distractedly stumbled after him. "What the hell could do that man?"

"I don't know, man. I just know something bad happened here, and we're never going to find out what it was, so I don't fucking care."

"Sarge, it'd take a fucking circus strongman with a machete to be able to get off someone's arm like that..."

"Corporal, stow that shit. The men and I are freaked out enough by this as it is. Let's just move on."

Hanson nodded, and the two of them jogged after the rest of the squad.

In the days to come, they would often think of the strange day in that clearing, and the more conclusions they came to, the less happy they were.

CHAPTER SIX

The next day they reached Hai Trang.

They had expected it to be small, but it was still smaller than any of them had imagined. There were six bamboo huts, gathered close to each other. You could have stood at the door of one, and hit every other hut with a thrown tennis ball. Handcarts and wheelbarrows were dotted around the short dirt paths connecting the simple buildings. Boxes, crates, bottles, all the normal signs of life that one took for granted were stacked up by doors, and in neat piles in gardens. It looked like a nice place to make a small, but honest, living out in the countryside - if one was so inclined.

It would have been delightful, if it wasn't so deathly silent.

"Where the fuck is everyone, man?" muttered Walton, around a cigar.

They had approached the village down a short, wooded slope, and had seen no signs of life since they had first spotted it in the distance. Hanson brought his rifle up, and thumbed off the safety. "Keep them peeled, everyone. This looks bad."

"There's no animals, man," whispered Bradley, the quietest that anyone in the squad had ever heard him. "This is supposed to be a farming village, right? Where are all the animals?"

Falconer unslung his own rifle and advanced past Bradley and off to the side. "Maybe they're rice farmers. Maybe they don't keep livestock."

"I ain't never seen a farm in 'Nam that didn't have at least a motherfucking goat wandering around," Bradley ranted under his breath. "This is fucked up, man. I'm telling you: Charlie got ahead of us and smoked the whole place out. Probably stuck his dick in the goat too, if I know those fuckers."

Reese clapped him on the back of the helmet as he passed him. "Watch our six, Bradley. If you fuck up, when we get back to base I'm flushing your stash."

"Oh, please, sarge, like you know where my fucking stash is."

"Duct taped to the back of your headboard."

"I'll be good."

With hand signals, Reese split the squad. Hanson, Falconer and Turner went to the left, Reese, Walton, Winters and Bradley went to the right.

Hanson led his team around behind the back and side of a rectangular building that looked as though it could be used as storage, maybe as a barn of some kind. The sun was up high in the sky, though it hadn't yet reached mid-day. The light was good. Cloud cover was minimal. The breeze was gentle. It was a good day to be in Vietnam; or, at least, it would be, if he wasn't in a combat zone. He pulled the butt of his rifle up to his chest and started edging sidesteps to swing around the front of the barn and see what they were dealing with.

The three of them came around the side at the same time. The front wall of the building was destroyed. Up along the left side, the wall was mostly intact, until it reached where the door was, at which point the destruction began. The door hung loosely, tattered on its hinges, and the wall on the entire right side was a tattered veil of bamboo, pulled and twisted in to shreds.

The sun streaked inside, and they could see rotting vegetables piled on tables, bags and bags of rice crawling with parasites. Against the wall on the far-side corner an old woman lay slumped. Blood saturated her dress and it was obvious she'd been dead for several days.

Falconer stepped slowly into the building, swinging his gaze left and right. He looked into the side of the building that was obscured by the remaining part of the wall and shouted back his findings. "More food. Two more dead. Two guys by the look of it. One's decapitated."

"Leave them," said Turner. "Could be wired."

Falconer nodded and stepped back into the sunlight. "What happened here, Hanson?"

Hanson was studying the tattered wall. He grabbed a section that was hanging, blowing in the wind a little. "This doesn't make sense. Look at the ground here. This wasn't pushed in, it was pulled out."

Turner looked at the ground. "Nah, the wind just blew the debris around."

"Even so, if they did knock it down, what did they knock it down with? There's no tyre tracks, and even if there was, Charlie doesn't have access to combat vehicles."

Falconer stepped back out and joined them. "You hear that?"

"Hear what?"

"Exactly. There's nothing. You can just about hear the wind out here. It's fucking eerie, man."

Turner rolled his eyes. "Pack that shit in, New Guy. This ain't the Haunted Mansion, all right? Gooks killed each other, and we found the mess they left behind, all right?"

Hanson gestured for them to keep quiet. "Keep it down, guys. The area isn't secure yet."

***

Winters was on point, and the first to find the dead animals. "Two pigs and a goat, sarge. They're like the guy we found."

Reese looked over Winters' shoulder, into the animal pen. "Bled out?"

"Looks like it, sergeant."

Bradley was looking around them. "Two guys over by the wall there. They look dead. You want me to check them out?"

"Leave them for now, but keep an eye on them. Maybe the motherfuckers are just playing dead."

Walton examined an overturned wheelbarrow. "This thing is riddled with bullet holes. Looks like small arms fire."

"You mean like an AK? Could Charlie have done this?"

Walton shook his head. "Too spaced out. It looks like it could have been an automatic pistol, but maybe it was just a six shooter fired real fast."

Reese looked around him. The other team was only fifty yards away. He'd been told Hai Trang was small and remote, but he hadn't been prepared for just *how* small and remote. He lit a cigarette and gestured for Walton to follow him to the next hut.

Walton stood ready with the huge M60 as Reese silently counted to three on his fingers then threw the door wide open. Even with the sun beating down it was pretty dark in there. Reese clicked on a torch and swept it around the room. This room was in pretty good order. Whatever had happened to the rest of the village had obviously not reached the inside of this particular hut. Pots and bowls were stacked neatly, clothes folded on a rudimentary bunk, a rice rug stretched across the floor. It was a simple life, but apparently a good one.

"Why smash the shit out of that barn down the road, kill everyone in the village and bleed out the livestock, but then leave this place untouched?" Walton asked.

"I don't know, man. Maybe whoever did this was disturbed and had to run off, before finding what they came for?"

"Viet Cong runs these lands, sarge. They don't answer to nobody."

"They'd run if a Thud or a Phantom came screaming by. They've learned to fear those babies." While the ground war in Vietnam was a messy, inconsistent affair, there was no doubt that the US forces ruled the skies. The NVAF had a few shitty Chinese MiG knock-offs to their name, but they just couldn't compete with the equipment or the training that the USAF and USN forces had.

Reese had an idea. He kicked the rice mat away, and smirked as his hunch was proven. In the middle of the floor was a small wooden trapdoor. 'Trapdoor' was a generous term, as it was no more than some nailed together slats of wood covering a hole in the earthen floor, but it served the same purpose. He quickly checked the timbers for any sign of wires or booby traps and, finding none, he threw back the covering.

There, inside the small hole, was a US forces radio in its protective case. "This is Doctor Bo Xuan's place. He's our man...wherever it is he's got to."

"You think he ran?" asked Walton. "You know what he looks like?"

Reese shook his head. "No. I mean, yes: he looks like an old Vietnamese man. There's nothing special about him. I got a photo, but if those bodies out there are in the condition those gooks in the clearing were, then I don't know that a Polaroid is going to do us much good, Walton."

Walton had already stepped back into the sunlight, and walked along to the next hut. "Some surface damage to the outside of this one, sarge. Doesn't look like it was shot up. Looks like someone was hacking at it with a machete or something."

Reese caught up and looked at what the gunner was pointing at. "So it does. Could have been a scythe or sickle or something. Both farmers and Charlie have lots of those to play with. He pushed open the door. "Empty. Again, no sign of disturbance."

"So if they weren't raiding, why'd they come here and kill everyone?"

Reese shrugged. "Who knows? If they suspected Doctor Xuan of colluding with us, then they sure as shit didn't find his radio."

"Doesn't mean shit with Charlie, sarge. They're fucking animals."

***

Winters and Bradley were still by the pig yard. Bradley took a gulp from his hip flask and offered it to Winters. "What you think is doing this, man? Some kinda disease or something?"

Winters accepted a swig. "I don't know."

"The hell you talking about, man? You've always got an idea about something. You're like a human calculator."

"I don't know. It's like no disease or animal attack I've ever heard of. The closest I can think of is how a spider feeds."

Bradley screwed the cap back onto the flask. "How do you mean, man?"

Winters was studying the animals that lay dead and drained in the mud. "A spider doesn't eat its prey. It drinks it. The venom that it uses to stun its prey also causes all of its organs and internal structure to break down and liquefy, and the spider then drinks the melted down contents."

"Okay, that explains the lack of blood, but bodies we've found so far still have their bones showing?"

"Most of the spiders we encounter only feed on invertebrates. They don't have an internal skeletal structure. Maybe their venom compound doesn't break down bone."

Bradley smiled, nervously. "You're a weird guy, you know that?"

"I read a lot."

"So, what are you saying? That a giant spider is doing all of this?"

"No, I'm not saying that at all. I said that this was the closest comparison I could come up with."

"Right."

"Besides, there's no webs anywhere. Very few spiders run down their prey."

Bradley hesitated half-way to lighting a cigarette. "That was a joke, right?"

"No."

***

Hanson, Falconer and Turner had found several more bodies, mostly men, though they had found a couple of young women together, crumpled and desiccated in the corner of a shack. One still had a pistol in her hands - an M1911 automatic; probably a gift from some visiting GI - or plundered from his dead body.

Their sweep complete, they were walking back down the main "street" (a very generous term) towards Reese and the rest of the squad, when they heard a noise from around the side of one of the shacks. Reese and Turner immediately brought their rifles up to their shoulder, and Falconer was only a fraction of a second behind them in doing so, but he took it as a painful reminder that he was still the Fucking New Guy. The three men cautiously sidestepped around the building, sighting along their rifles, scared even to blink in case someone should rush them.

Propped up against the wall were several crates and an overturned wheelbarrow. The men kept their rifles trained on the wooden boxes, which were twitching slightly.

Falconer felt adrenaline flood his body, a cold electric thrill that ran through all his muscles and nerve endings, making him aware that he was one hundred per cent totally and completely alive, and that this thing was happening in front of him *right now*.

The crates shifted up and down, as though something living and breathing were underneath them. Reese held up a palm, gesturing for them to stay back as he approached the shifting pile. Turner and Falconer kept their rifles trained on the movement, but held their ground, advancing no further. A shout drifted up from the other end of the village, but it was inaudible. They didn't know if they were just acknowledging that they'd noticed them and the crates, or if they were trying to alert them to a discovery of their own. It didn't matter right now, of course. All that mattered was keeping their guns trained on the moving boxes.

Reese reached out a hand and the stack shifted up and down again. Something - or someone - was definitely under there. Reese flashed a glance back at them to make sure that they had their guns ready, and then pulled back the top box.

A flash of white and a disgruntled huffing sound revealed a disturbed porcupine, who had apparently been hunting for scraps or picking up some of the bugs that were drawn to the rotting produce. Reese let out a sigh of relief - and gave a slight smile at how kind-of cute the porcupine was - and Turner and Falconer lowered their rifles.

An explosion of noise and movement made them yelp and snap their rifles up in alarm. The inverted wheelbarrow at the other side of the alleyway was thrown up and backwards. A young Vietnamese girl, no more than twenty years old, bolted past them. They had a fleeting glimpse of a white shirt and black pants, bare feet striking the mud, before she was clear of their reach and running down the central area towards the other fire team. Falconer was the first to recover and chase after her, throwing his rifle back on its shoulder strap. He could normally have caught her easily, but she had a head start and he was weighed down by combat and camping gear.

As she ran towards Reese's team, her foot struck a sod of earth, or perhaps some debris from the damaged barn and she pitched forward onto the muddy ground, catching herself with the palms of her hands. Falconer reached her at the same time Winters did; the radio operator must have been running towards her from the other side, Falconer hadn't even noticed. She rolled over onto her back, and they saw the dirt, rain water and dried blood that covered her hair and face.

Winters spoke to her in Vietnamese, firmly and clearly. Her eyes widened and she looked up and around at them as the rest of the squad arrived to stand around her. Her gaze focused on them, and she began to cry. It was a small child's cry, full of pain, confusion and rage against the injustice of the world. It was a cry none of them ever forgot, the cry of an adult completely broken.

A clap of thunder broke across the sky, and the rain began to fall.

PART TWO

PAINT IT BLACK

CHAPTER SEVEN

They carried the girl into the barn, and carried the dead woman out. As soon as the rain stopped, Reese intended to burn the bodies, along with the whole town if possible. As far as they could establish, this girl was the only survivor.

They sat her up against the wall and tried their best to calm her while the storm raged outside. Walton and Falconer set up a small stove to make coffee and to heat rations, while Turner and Bradley stood watch at the smashed up wall. It was a pretty futile exercise. Cloud cover had come across the sky exceedingly quickly, and the rain was so thick it was like gazing through television static.

"You see anything, man?" Bradley asked, cupping his cigarette in his hand, shielding it from the wind and rain.

"Man, I see everything and nothing."

"What do you mean?"

"There ain't nothing out there but rain and trash. I know that; but I see Charlie everywhere. As soon as you think you'll never be able to see them, that's when they'll get you. Always keep looking, man. Stay cool, you know what I'm saying?"

"Yeah. Sounds like you're saying you're fucking paranoid, man."

Bradley chuckled. "Hey, that's fine by me, man. Paranoid guys stay alive. When you're in country, you stay paranoid as long as you can."

"Amen, man."

Reese was standing over the girl, while Winters and Hanson - the two Vietnamese language speakers in the squad - squatted down next to her, trying to communicate. The language always sounded strange and alien like to the Sergeant. It was a jumble of twanging "n" sounds, and protracted hollow vowels. It wasn't like French or German, in which you could hear the odd word that sounded familiar. It was a wholly different sound.

The woman had - so far, at least - been unable to respond. After her initial bout of infant-like crying, she had become almost catatonic. Reese was hoping that the warmth, some food and some sleep may help to bring her out of it, but he wasn't especially confident. He'd seen combat fatigue ("Shell Shock" was what they used to call it) several times, and this woman had a bad case of it. Whatever happened here had been bad enough to take her mind to the brink of snapping.

Hanson stood up, and whispered to him, while Winters continued trying to communicate. "I can't get anything out of her. Winters speaks much better Vietnamese than I do. Is there anything else I can be doing, because I feel like a fifth wheel doing this?"

"I don't know, is there anything else you can do?"

"Is there any reason for us to stick around in Hai Trang longer than we need to? We think the doctor is dead, right?"

Reese lit a cigarette and nodded. "I'm pretty sure he's the older guy we found, but I can't say for sure. The body was hardly in the best condition."

"Right. How about I take the map and sort out our route out of here? It doesn't seem fair to give Walton the same gig twice, and I'd rather avoid cutting back across that clearing again."

"Man, after this village, the clearing doesn't seem all that bad, does it?"

Hanson shook his head. "The clearing was weird, man. Eerie. None of us want to go back that way."

Reese huffed out a sigh and took another drag on his cigarette. "What do you think we're dealing with here?"

"It's either the Viet Cong, vampires, or Viet Cong vampires."

"Sounds like shit you'd see Winters reading."

"I know." Hanson suppressed a shiver as a gust of wind howled past the opening in the wall. "What do you think happened?"

"I don't have a better guess, so I'm going with Viet Cong Vampires."

Winters stood and interrupted them. "She's asleep. I couldn't get much out of her. From what I could get, I think she was working for Doctor Xuan. A nurse, maybe. Her name is Lai Anh."

Reese and Hanson looked over to where the girl was sleeping. "Any theories about what happened here, Winters?" Reese asked.

Winters looked at Hanson. "Did you tell him about the Viet Cong Vampires?"

Hanson suppressed a giggle with the back of his hand. "Yeah. Yeah, I did, Private."

Winters wasn't laughing. "I've got nothing else. I'd like to take a look at some of the dead bodies before we cremate them. If I get a better idea as to the cause of death then maybe I can come up with a better working theory."

Reese shrugged. "You wanna poke around with a dead gook then, please, be my guest."

"Thank you, sergeant."

"Remember the dead Viet Cong we found in the clearing?" Hanson asked, catching Winters as he was already turning to leave.

"Of course."

"Do you think that whatever happened to the villagers here is what happened to him?"

"Well, as I said, I'd need more time with the villagers here, but…yes. I think that's a pretty safe guess."

"Thank you, Private," said Reese. "Go help the others with the food. Corporal Hanson and I will watch the girl."

Winters nodded and went to join the others.

A flash of lightning caused shouts from Bradley and Turner at the opening. Reese and Hanson rushed over to them. Hanson had his M1911 sidearm ready, and Reese cursed under his breath for running in without any weapon. He was more tired than he'd thought. Bradley had dropped to a squatting position, rifle to his shoulder, Turner stood, rifle raised shouting for whoever he had seen to freeze.

"What is it?" shouted Reese. "What do you see?"

Bradley had to shout to be heard over the thunder that crackled and rolled across them. "I don't know, sarge! I just saw movement, running low. Could have been someone crawling. Could have been an animal. I don't know!"

They watched for several minutes before Bradley lowered his gun, feeling a little embarrassed. "I don't see anything, now. Maybe it was just the lightning, making it look like something was crawling along the ground. It was weird, though. It moved strangely. Maybe it was- ah, I don't know. I'm sorry. Maybe I just got spooked."

Hanson lowered his gun. "That's okay, Private. We'll switch you two over with Walton and Falconer. Go grab yourself some rest."

***

They mashed the rations together to make an acceptable stew. It wasn't exactly delicious, but it was warm and filling, which was what they needed.

It was another three hours before Lai Anh woke up. Winters was the first to notice, and took her over his mess tin loaded up with some of the stew, and a cup of coffee. She looked at him warily, but her hunger got the better of her caution and she accepted the food gratefully. She was momentarily confused by the fork he offered her, and she had to watch the others eating for a while to understand what she was supposed to do with it.

After she had eaten most of the food, she smiled at him, and bowed a little.

"Lai Anh," he spoke to her in Vietnamese. "Do you know what happened to the people here?"

Reese and Walton were asleep, but Hanson, roused by the quiet sound of their voices, came and sat next to them, nodding and smiling at the girl.

Lai Anh's eyes glazed over for a moment, and she shivered before nodding. She spoke a few words in Vietnamese that Hanson didn't understand. Winters looked similarly confused.

"Do you understand her?" he asked.

"I...think so. I think she said it was a beast. A beast of the jungle."

Hanson's arm hairs rose. He liked a spooky B-movie as much as the next man, but watching some hokey black and white creature feature with your friends in a drive-in was very different to sitting in a storm, halfway around the world, surrounded by dead men. "You mean like a tiger or something? Could she mean a tiger?"

Winters turned back to her. "Hổ?"

The woman shook her head and said "Rết."

"What was that? What does that mean?" Hanson asked.

Winters shook his head. "I don't know. I've not heard it before. It doesn't sound like any word I know, either."

"I thought you were fluent in this?"

"No, Corporal. I just know more than anyone else in the squad, which makes me the de facto expert."

Hanson nodded. "Yeah, I know how that works. Ask her if this beast has a name."

Winters spoke to her rapidly. She nodded and replied, "Việt Nam Đen."

Winters nodded, and turned back to Hanson. "That means-"

"I know what it means."

The girl started talking again. At first her speech came in bits and pieces, but as she gathered momentum she began to talk faster and louder, as though a small leak in a dam had gradually forced its way through until the water came in a gushing spout.

Winters struggled to keep up, but never broke from his monotone deadpan. "The animals died first. Each morning, there would be one or two dead. Chickens first. No heads. Then one of the old women was found."

Lai Anh fell silent at this.

"Found desiccated. Like the others?"

"I assume so. They found her outside the village. Apparently there's a well or something uphill from here. The woman went to get water, and never returned. The following morning, they found her. She was..."

Winters looked confused.

"Winters? What was she?"

Winters showing confusion was unnerving. Hanson had always mentally compared him to Mister Spock from the television show *Star Trek*. Winters was unemotional, detached and analytical. He was also - hands down - the smartest one in the squad. He had the kind of brain that just seemed to soak up trivia and information, so if you needed to know something weird and specific, asking Winters was always quicker than looking it up yourself. If it had been any other day, then seeing Winters foxed would have been downright weird. On top of everything else they had already discovered, it was almost unearthly. Hanson was really starting to feel like he'd stumbled into an episode of *The Twilight Zone*.

Private Winters blinked away the confusion and said, "I think she said that she was…hollow?"

Lai Anh had started talking again, and Winters was listening closely. Hanson tried to break down what the girl could have meant. Did she mean gutted? Decomposed? "Winters, could she mean desiccated, like the Viet Cong we found out in the clearing?"

Winters didn't answer straight away, waiting for the girl to finish speaking. "Two men from the village went hunting for what could have done this to the woman. They never returned. More livestock went missing or were…hollowed. Yes, sarge, I think it's safe to assume she means desiccated."

"So what's doing this? Some kind of animal?"

"Yes, sarge. The Việt Nam Đen."

***

They were awake at sunrise, watching the sun change from black to a yellow-orange as the day broke. Falconer hefted his pack onto his back, and kept one eye on Lai Anh, who was leaning against one of the huts, staring at the floor. He wished he had something he could say to comfort her, but he had failed - rather spectacularly - to learn any Vietnamese at all. He'd been terrible with languages, and had consistently flunked Spanish at high school.

Walton clapped him on the shoulder and smiled. "Pretty, ain't she?"

"Aw, come on, man. She's a kid."

"So are you, New Guy."

"Hey, I'm not a kid, I'm twenty years old."

Walton laughed loudly and hefted the large M60 rifle up. "Well, excuse me, grandpa!"

Turner and Bradley heard this and joined in the laughter, and Falconer blushed even redder than the sun and heat had already made him. For the rest of his time in Vietnam, he was known - somewhat affectionately - as Grandpa, and while it wasn't the coolest nickname he could have hoped for, he was relieved that he was no longer the Fucking New Guy.

Reese spoke clearly and loudly to all of them. "Okay, people, listen up. I'm saying that Doctor Xuan is missing, presumed dead; most likely as the result of a Viet Cong attack. I take it there's no-one here who wants to question that?"

Winters went to speak, but Reese noticed and cut him off.

"I don't much care for the testimony of the Princess over there. You bring me a hysterical little girl talking about monsters that come out of the jungle in the night, then I'm going to be a little skeptical, okay? We're taking her back with us, and Military Intelligence can talk to her, and decide where she goes next, okay? She can't stay here, because this place is a goddamned ghost town."

"You want to torch the place, sarge?" Bradley asked.

Reese waved his hand. "No, I don't want to make that kind of call, and those weren't my orders. If they want it destroyed they can send in the Phantoms. Hanson here has worked out our return journey. Corporal?"

"I'm looping us back around. Given the dead bodies we found, not to mention the booby trap, I think we're all keen to avoid that road. We're lopping around, following a trail, and then there's a river tributary we can follow. It'll add another day to the journey, but it'll be an easy walk, and should be clear of Charlie, which is something we all need."

"Is the girl coming with us willingly?" Falconer asked.

"I've told her she has no choice, and she's shown no intention of opposing us," said Winters. "I'm happy to volunteer to keep a hold of her."

"That's probably the best idea," said Sergeant Reese. "No-one speaks gook like you do, anyway."

"Thank you, sarge. I try hard."

"Okay, move out."

With mutterings and grumblings, the squad pulled on their packs and rifles and followed Hanson (who was on point, for now) away from the little town of Hai Trang, and out into the jungle.

***

They had been walking for a couple of hours when the first bullet struck the ground near Hanson's feet. He felt the impact, then time slowed down for a half a second, before he heard the crack of the shot. He swore and staggered backwards, falling into the undergrowth. The rest of the squad shouted an alarm and ducked behind trees, or dropped to lay along the path, keeping their eyes peeled for any sign of their attacker.

Lai Anh had yelped and burst into tears, burying her face into Winters' chest, the normally stoic man placing an arm around her and slinging his rifle for his M1911 sidearm.

"How many?" Bradley shouted to Hanson.

Hanson squinted through the jungle around them. "I don't fucking see any, man. Could be one, could be a hundred."

CHAPTER EIGHT

Reese called across to Walton. "Walton, did you see where the shots came from?"

"No, sarge!" the large man replied, and pointed uphill and across from them. "There's a ridge up there, that's a good bet, but I couldn't say for sure, sarge."

Another round cracked into one of the trees they were cowering behind. "That's a bolt action rifle!" shouted Bradley. "Charlie uses them when they can't get AKs."

Hanson had recovered a little, and was now prone in the undergrowth, sighting along his rifle in the direction the shots had come from. The shots were coming slowly and infrequently, which suggested to him that there was only one shooter. This was good news because it meant they weren't getting suppressive fire from twenty or so psychotic Viet Cong, but it was bad news because one man was considerably harder to spot than twenty. He swept his gaze back and forth across the zone he thought that the shots had come from, desperate to spot any signs of movement.

Falconer felt his heart hammering in his chest. "Where the fuck is he?" he whispered to himself. "Where the fuck is he?"

"Easy, Grandpa...don't let him get to you," Turner whispered back.

A round struck the bark of the tree right by Falconer's face and he screamed as the hot wood splinters peppered his cheek. Convinced he'd been hit, he fell onto his backside, slapping his palm to his face and being surprised to find only stubble.

"I saw the flash!" called Walton, and everyone jumped as the M60 barked into life. Rounds poured into a copse of trees up the slope and to their right, shredding bracken and leaves, the sound echoing up and around the previously still jungle. Turner and Hanson provided supporting fire. After about three seconds, they all cut off their attack, and watched still for a moment.

No motion came from the bushes or grass in the copse. The only sound was Lai Anh whimpering against Winters.

Falconer was checked over hurriedly by Bradley, and they both shared a smile and a laugh of relief when they saw he was completely unscathed, and how lucky he had been to be just centimetres from a fatal head shot.

They waited a full ten minutes, hunched over and uncomfortable and damp, and there was no movement, and no more shots coming from the trees. Reese gestured with a hand-signal, and Turner and Walton stepped forward toward the shooter's location, advancing slowly, guns raised. The rest of the squad watched around them, looking for any sign of movement from other shooters. There was every chance this whole set up had been a trap and that a VC brigade was about to jump out of the trees.

The two men reached the suspected location of the sniper, and looked into it for a moment. Walton looked back and waved that it was all clear.

"Gook must be dead," muttered Bradley. "Good fucking riddance. Motherfucker take a shot at me, the motherfucker better be ready to die."

Reese and Hanson came over to join them. Their suspicions were correct. The man was wearing the "pyjamas" typical of a Viet Cong soldier. At least six rounds had found their mark, and he was already dead, still bleeding onto the jungle floor. At his feet was a scuffed and battered Lee Enfield rifle. Reese didn't know where a Vietnamese civilian could have gotten a British WWII rifle from, but there it was. There was some rice and a bottle of what he assumed was water - or moonshine - a couple of feet over. The man had obviously been watching the path for some time, waiting for US or ARVN forces to come by, and take pot shots at them.

"Well, one down, another hundred thousand to go..." muttered Walton, lighting a cigar.

"There may be more," said Hanson, picking up the Lee Enfield, and examining it. "One buwwet left," he said with a Bugs Bunny voice.

"You think there might be a tunnel system?" asked Turner.

Reese shrugged. "It's possible. The ARVN guys we bumped into the other day certainly seemed to think so. If there is, it'd go some way to explaining how they'd done such a number in Hai Trang and disappeared so quickly."

"You think we should go looking?"

"Yeah. Yeah, I do." He looked back and waved for the rest of the squad to join them. "Okay, lads, ladies and Bradley, fan out and search the area for any signs of Charlie. Watch for traps, and keep them peeled. You know the score. Winters, you can leave the little lady here with Hanson and I."

Winters nodded and passed the girl to Hanson, who seemed reluctant at first, but relaxed when Hanson was able to speak a few words to her in Vietnamese.

"Ah, Jesus...*fuck*!" shouted Turner. "Sarge, there's more here!"

"More what, Private?"

"Fucking body parts, sir. I just damn near fell over a fucking body!"

Reese nodded to Hanson and the corporal headed over to see what it was Turner had discovered.

Turner was standing only a few feet away, and looked like he was suppressing the urge to vomit. Reese looked down at a naked, dead man. Not only was he decapitated, but all four limbs looked as though they had all been mangled and mauled about with some sort of wicked bladed farming equipment.

"There's hardly any blood," said Turner. "Look, there's some spray on the leaves, but nowhere what you'd expect for an attack like this. He should be swimming in a fucking pool of blood. It's fucking dry, man."

Hanson prodded the corpse with his boot. "He's been dead a while. There's some fucked up animal life out here that could've been eating it. Drinking up the blood, maybe. I don't know."

"There's a severed arm over here," called Winters. "Desiccated, like the bodies back at Hai Trang."

"Lot of blood up against this tree over here, man," Walton yelled. "Something went down here, and once again, I don't think Charlie did too well out of it. It's kind of like that clearing we found the dead guy in, remember?"

"Dead goat," called Winters.

"What?" shouted Reese, uncertain he'd heard him right.

Winters turned to face him and shrugged. "Dead goat."

"The fuck is a goat doing all the way out here?"

Winters shrugged again, confused at the inanity of the question. "Maybe they used her for milk. They could have taken it in the raid of Hai Trang, if that was Charlie. It's dead now."

"How bad is the body?"

Winters raised an eyebrow. "I don't understand what you mean, sarge."

"Is it mangled? Clean kill? How old is it?"

"It's…yeah, it's…it's pretty mangled, sir. Lacerations, some down to the bone. Bled out. Head is partially hanging off. The animals vent is…cored."

"Say what? Grandpa, get over there and help Winters."

Falconer jogged over to where the radio operator stood, looked down, turned his head and vomited.

"That bad, huh?" asked Reese.

Falconer was doubled over, hands on his knees, panting for breath. "It's pretty bad, sarge. It's partially eaten."

Winters nodded. "I can't tell if it was eaten pre or post mortem. Sadly, that's not exactly one of my skill sets. I'll have to read up on that next chance I get."

Falconer ignored him and shouted back to Reese. "Whatever started eating this ate it from the asshole up, sarge. And they…it's like they ate all the meat and organs, but left the bone and the skin. Mostly. It's got a pretty fucked up asshole, sarge."

"That's what I said," muttered Winters, poking at the corpse with his bayonet. "It's been cored."

Walton was walking slowly around a small group of trees. "Guys, this area's pretty good for a tunnel system. If Charlie was going to build one it's the perfect soil, the perfect location…hell, I'd say there's got to be one around here."

He looked around at the base of the trees, at the roots, hoping to see some sign of tunnelling having taken place. He couldn't see any overturned earth, uneven rocks or debris that could be used to conceal a cave entrance. What he did find, however, was a strange reddish brown smear, running down the tree. At first he thought it was some sort of resin the tree was secreting, but when he saw the flies and insects' interest in it, he realised it was dried blood, and partially dried shit. He snapped his gaze upwards, into the branches, and locked eyes with the oily, dead gaze of a decomposing Viet Cong corpse. He fell onto his backside with a scream, instinctively snatching his sidearm from his belt, and was still shouting at the cadaver when Hanson and Turner arrived. Turner helped the large man back up while Hanson studied the body.

"Another Viet Cong?" asked Turner.

"Yeah, going on the uniform and the AK. A girl, from the haircut," Hanson replied.

"How the hell did she get up there?"

"She climbed."

Walton was gradually composing himself. "You mean she climbed up there and then bled out?"

"I guess so. I mean, I can't see any obvious wounds, so who knows what caused it? She could've been shot or stabbed, and climbed up there to escape."

Turner shook his head. "No way, man. She's only about eight feet off of the ground. Bitch didn't evade anyone by only being eight feet off of the goddamn ground."

Hanson shrugged. "You wanna go up there and get a better look at her?"

"No, man. I think YOU should go up there and get a better look at her."

"Fuck this mission, man…" muttered Walton.

"What the hell is doing this?" asked Hanson, only half to himself.

Turner slung his rifle and shrugged. "I don't give a shit any more, man. I just want to get out of here. Fuck this jungle, fuck this mission and fuck this war, man."

Walton was still looking at the dead girl. "Do you think it followed her up there, or do you think she got up there to die?"

"Both. Maybe. I don't know," said Hanson. "Let's get the fuck out of here. Regroup on the sarge."

The three of them left the mystery girl in the tree to the wind and the bugs. Just another story from Vietnam without a beginning or an end.

***

"If there's a tunnel system, then it's close," Sergeant Reese informed them. "If it's close, then we should investigate. Pair up. Have a nose around. Keep them peeled for any sign of a tunnel network, or Charlie himself."

"What exactly are we looking for, sarge?" asked Falconer.

"Well, a tunnel opening would be a lovely thing to stumble across, but Charlie is usually too smart just to leave them hanging open like a whore's legs. Look for odd looking rocks, misplaced topsoil, wooden debris working as a trapdoor. If you think it looks suspicious, check it for tripwires, then try moving it. If there's a tunnel underneath then, well done, you found a gook tunnel."

"Yes, sarge."

"I'll stay here with the girl. Winters and Hanson. Turner and Falconer. Walton and Bradley."

"Aw, sarge," Walton rolled his eyes melodramatically, "how come I get Bradley? Ain't we got some colouring in he can do instead?"

The squad laughed and Bradley playfully slapped the big man on the arm. "Fuck you, man. My brains and your brawn are the perfect team."

"Ain't nothing wrong with my brains, little man. What's wrong with your brawn?"

Hanson and Winters headed off to the north side of the ridge. When they were a distance away that they couldn't be overheard, Hanson told Winters about the dead girl in the branches, and asked him what he thought might have happened.

"Bradley was asking me similar questions back in the village. I've been thinking on it, and there are several animals that practice hematophagy"-

"Homowhatnow?"

"Hematophagy. Feeding on blood. That's the only explanation I can come up with for how the bodies we've found so far have been so heavily desiccated. Lampreys, leeches and, of course, vampire bats. The former are too small to have the impact that we've witnessed so far, and I don't even know if vampire bats live in Vietnam. If they do, then we'd certainly have noticed a swarm large enough to take out a village and two Viet Cong outposts."

"Right. How about spiders? Don't they feed on blood?"

"Not exactly. They bite their prey and vomit digestive fluid into their prey. This liquifies all their insides, and they suck that up."

Hanson stopped and felt his arm hairs rise. "So, what you're saying is it could be spiders? Some kind we haven't come across before?"

Winters shrugged. "That would have to be a big spider now, wouldn't it?"

"Or swarm."

Winters shook his head. "Spiders are solitary. Otherwise they'd just eat each other."

Hanson was always surprised by just how much the robot-like radio operator knew about seemingly obscure topics. "How the hell do you always know this stuff, Winters?"

"I read a lot."

"About the dietary habits of spiders?"

Winters shrugged. "About lots of things. I like learning."

"Well, that is admirable. Hey, you see that?"

Hanson pointed to a curious, humped part of the soil. They raised their rifles and approached it cautiously, sidestepping around it until they reached the far side.

The dark mouth of a tunnel greeted them. A pile of messy, wooden slats lay to the side, which obviously served as a door or cover for the entrance. Hanson called over to the rest of the squad. "Hey, over here! We found a tunnel!"

Winters squatted down, and flashed his torch into it. "It goes back a fair way, then looks like it slopes downwards a little. Charlie likes to dig some really complex tunnels, so I couldn't guess at how far it goes, or how large it is."

"Or if it's occupied."

"Unlikely, but it's impossible to say for sure."

Hanson waved his arm to Reese and gestured that he should head over to them.

He was looking forward to showing off his find, when the sound of Walton and Bradley shouting for assistance drifted across on the wind.

CHAPTER NINE

Winters and Hanson hurried back in the direction they had come, leaping over branches and the occasional Viet Cong body. Hanson's heart felt like a machine gun in his chest; he knew that at any moment either he or Winters could stumble into a pit trap, or set off a trip wire, and at least one of them would be down and out for the count. He knew that the rational thing to do was to advance slowly and carefully to assist Bradley and Walton; but in his heart he knew that time was of the essence and he would rather die trying to help than live with knowing he could have gotten to help them in time. Ahead of them, he could see Sergeant Reese dragging Lai Anh in the direction of the shouts, and Turner and Falconer running, coming in from a right angle.

Now, close by a copse of trees he could see Bradley standing, waving them over, while Walton sat on his backside on the floor, leaning back and supporting his weight on the palms of his hands. As they got closer, Hanson could see that the situation was bad.

Reese reached them first, sliding onto his knees at Walton's side, studying his leg. Now that they were only about thirty yards away, Hanson could see that one of Walton's legs was sunk up to the knee in a pit trap. Walton was gritting his teeth against the pain.

As soon as they reached them, Winters fell into a defensive position, pulling the butt of his rifle up to his shoulder and scanning the trees and surrounding area, knowing that the whole point of this pit trap could be to distract the squad so that Viet Cong forces could ambush them - an attack that could be especially effective with the M60 operator temporarily out of action. The M60 spat out bullets at a terrifying rate and could provide very effective suppressing fire, which would force any attacking force to think twice about sticking their heads up to take a shot. It had dealt very effectively with the sniper not even an hour earlier.

Hanson crouched down and studied the pit trap. It was a small hole, barely even eighteen inches wide, but the inside had been lined with twenty or so vicious looking stakes, sloping downwards at forty five degrees. The damp and the rain had gotten to them, so the tips weren't as sharp as they had been when the pit trap was first dug. They had still managed to rip some holes into his combat trousers, however, and the edges of the holes were bloodstained.

"Is it bad?" asked Walton. "It doesn't feel too bad, but I can't see shit."

"I'll have to take a closer look, but it looks okay so far," said Hanson, grabbing a torch from his bag. Even in the bright sunlight, it was pretty dark down there, being so small and mostly blocked up with Walton's leg.

Falconer and Turner skidded to a halt next to them, and Reese gestured for them to join Winters in keeping watch on the surrounding area.

Hanson peered down into the hole with the torch. It looked like the stakes had only just scratched Walton's leg, so he should be okay to walk. Furthermore, it didn't look like they'd been coated with anything unpleasant. Obviously this was an amateur job - although he wouldn't tell Walton that. The big man would be embarrassed to have been caught by a hack job.

"It's not too bad, big man. Don't try and pull, though. The stakes are angled, so they'll cut you to shit if you try. I'll have to dig them out."

"Aw, fuck, man."

"Sarge, can you and the boys keep watch? This could take some time."

"How long, Corporal?"

Hanson shrugged. "At least ten minutes; maybe half an hour. Depends how long the stakes are and how well they're sunk in. Could be a big job."

Walton groaned again, more from frustration than pain. "Fucking gook motherfuckers. If the son of a bitch who dug this is still alive, I'll fucking gut him myself."

Winters swung his rifle around sharply at some movement in the vegetation behind them. It hadn't sounded like slow deliberate movement like someone sneaking up on them, or even a stalking jungle cat, would make. It sounded more like a rush and scurry, like that of a prey animal. It could have been a porcupine, like the one they found back at the village, he supposed. It could even have been a bird of some sort.

Something about the noise had unnerved him, though. It seemed to drag on for longer than one would have expected. It was an elongated susurrus of sibilant movement, rather than the barge and rush of something small. He wondered if it might have been a snake, but he didn't really know much about the local snakes. It was an odd thing him not to know, he thought, making a mental note to read up about them the next chance he got.

He watched the area for a count of ten, and when there were no more signs or sounds of movement, he turned back to scanning other parts of the woods.

Hanson was hacking away at the small stakes with his combat knife. A couple of them had folding shovels on their backpacks, but there simply wasn't the room to work with one. Walton's muscular build was usually an advantage, but right now the beefcake was just plugging up the hole. He reached the base of one of the stakes and wiggled it out like a loose tooth. It was about eight inches long, which meant that only three inches or so of each stake was buried.

"They're not buried too deep. We should have him out in ten minutes. Maybe fifteen. The stakes are clean, too. No shit or anything worse on them."

"Let's be grateful for small mercies," muttered Sergeant Reese. "You work on digging the big lug out."

"Yes, sarge. Oh, when Winters and I were back over there, we found a tunnel entrance." He paused to lever another stake from the wall of the pit. "It looks like it runs deep, but we didn't get much of a chance to look far into it. I'd say it's definitely Charlie."

"Unoccupied?"

"Couldn't say, sarge. Weirdest thing, though - the cover was just hanging off of it."

"So? What makes that strange?"

Another stake was thrown onto the ground with a thud. "Well, if there was someone alive in there, wouldn't they have pulled the cover back over the entrance? Seems to me that'd just be common goddamn sense."

Reese lit a cigarette as another stake was thrown past his boot. Walton joined in the conversation. "So, that should mean everyone inside is dead, right? No big deal."

"Hell of an assumption to make, Private," the sergeant replied. "And looking at you right now, I don't think we'll be taking your advice on whether it's okay or not to assume something."

"I'm just happy to be here, sarge."

The work was a lot quicker than Hanson had first estimated, and Walton was able to work his leg free in just another five minutes. Apart from some rips to his combats, and a few sore scratches here and there, he'd come out of the trap unscathed. Once he was free, he stood up and smashed in the remaining spikes with the butt of his M60. It was part prevention and part retribution.

Reese checked his watch. It was two thirty in the afternoon already, and they hadn't made much progress beyond Hai Trang. Hell, he could probably throw a tennis ball and still hit it. He'd hoped to have been long gone by now, but at the same time, he simply couldn't ignore the presence of a Viet Cong construction. "Ah, hell, let's go check this thing out. Can't leave Charlie a bolt hole to play in."

They fell into line and followed Hanson back to where he and Winters had found the entrance to the tunnel. Winters was at the rear, handling Lai Anh, and couldn't stop himself from throwing the odd glance back in the direction of the bushes, which he could have sworn he'd seen move again.

Turner raised an eyebrow at him. "You okay, bro? You look spooked."

"Yeah. Maybe a little, I guess. I don't know."

"That's fucking weird."

Winters blinked. "What is?"

"I've seen a lot of weird shit in this country, man, but I honestly never thought I'd see that."

Turner pulled a cigarette from the packet in his front pocket. "I never thought I'd fucking see you spooked, man."

***

It took them less than five minutes to reach the entrance to the tunnel. Straight away, Sergeant Reese squatted down and flashed his torch around the interior. The beam played off the rough earth within, and a damp smell wafted out. "Yeah, man. Gook tunnel. Can almost smell the rice."

Falconer squatted next to him, watching the torch play around the interior. "How big do you reckon it is?"

Reese shrugged. "They're as big or as small as they need them to be. One guy guarding an ammo dump may be a dug-out barely ten feet across. Then again, back a few years ago, they found a VC tunnel system underneath Saigon that they reckoned ran for seventy-five miles or more. When Gooks get determined, they get busy."

"Right. So, how large is this one?"

"Who knows? We don't know what it's for, or why it was made in the first place, how many gooks it was supposed to house…it's a mystery, Grandpa."

Falconer stood back up. "So, what do we do?"

Reese dusted his hands off, stood up and looked at the rest of the squad. "Okay, we've found a Gook tunnel. That means it's our duty to investigate it and find out what there is to be found. Normally we could make excuses, or even just pretend that we never saw it in the first place, because who would be any the wiser, right?"

A chorus of muttered agreements answered him.

"Unfortunately for us, this time it does matter. Our mission was to investigate what happened to Dr Xuan, and the village of Hai Trang, and it's pretty obvious to me that the occupants of this tunnel were what happened to them. That means we've got to investigate the tunnels."

Turner raised his hand, a strange hangover from High School that never seemed to have left him. "Sorry, sarge, but we don't have the right equipment or the right number of men for this. We don't even have a flame-thrower. I don't want to go into one of those god damn bug houses without a burner, sarge. Hell, we should wait for a goddamn Fire-Track."

"I'm aware of our situation, Turner, but that doesn't change the fact this is a job that needs doing. Now, you're right. We don't have flame or gas, and we've only got a handful of smokers that I'd much rather hang onto in case we need to call in a chopper."

"We don't need to clear it out," said Hanson, quietly. "We just need to investigate it. We just need to get an idea of the tunnels, and what we think they're being used for. If the brass decide that it's worth investigating, then they can send someone else with the right equipment next time."

Reese nodded. "All right. What do you suggest, Corporal?"

"Two guys. Leave their rifles and armour out here; they'll only hold them up in the tunnels. Torch each, pistol each, and go in quickly and quietly to scout it out."

"You volunteering, Corporal?" Walton asked, with a smile.

Hanson pulled a face. "You've seen the size of the tunnel, right? We're going to have to send in someone a little smaller."

Everyone turned simultaneously to the shortest, skinniest member of the squad: Private Darterrius Bradley. "Aw, fuck you guys," he muttered. "Why you always picking on me?"

"We're not picking on you, Bradley," said Sergeant Reese. "This is pure practicality - and this is a mission for which God and Mother Nature have deemed you perfectly sized for."

"Fuck. Fine. You know what? Fine. If I'm gonna die, why not have it be in a fucking worm infested hole that stinks of Gook shit, right? Fuck this war, man."

"Who goes in with him?" asked Turner.

Hanson nodded in the direction of Winters. "Winters is the next smallest. He should go."

Bradley nodded. "Yeah, send Winters. At least he's fucking sharp and can watch my back, unlike some dumb motherfuckers who'll stick their foot in every Gook trap they can find."

Walton flipped him off. "Fuck you, man."

"Winters stays here," said the Sergeant. "He's the only one capable of talking to Lai Anh and I want to have another conversation with her before the day is out."

Bradley looked around at the squad, and the realisation slowly dawned on him. "You mean I'm taking the Fucking New Guy in with me? No way, man. He ain't ready for this shit. No disrespect, Grandpa, but you're fucking new here. Sarge, he don't know what to look for. He don't know what to expect."

Reese's expression hardened. He grabbed Bradley by the shirt, and loomed right in his face. "Private Alex Falconer here is a goddamn US soldier, Private. He will fight and die by your side, because that's what soldiers do, and you'll do the goddamn best you can by him in return. Do I make myself abso-fucking-lutely clear on this, you dense motherfucker? You two are going to get your asses into that tunnel, you're going to dig around, and you're going to come back here with the fucking Encyclopedia Gook-tannica on what's going on in there. Do you understand me, Private?"

Private Bradley paled, and the entire rest of the squad had fallen silent. They'd never seen Sergeant Reese flip his lid like that before. They'd seen Bradley wind everyone up again and again - even in the most dangerous of circumstances, but they honestly didn't think anything would ever come of it...least of all Bradley.

Reese slowly relaxed his grip on Bradley's uniform, and the Private stepped shakily backwards. "Yes. Yes, sarge. We'll go in there. We'll go in there. Okay?"

Reese nodded to Winters. "The corporal, you and I need to talk to Miss Lai Anh. If she's calmed down a little by now, who knows, she might remember something a little more useful to us. The rest of you, keep watch, and listen out for Bradley and Grandpa."

Winters nodded.

Bradley handed his rifle to Turner, checked his pistol, and nodded to Falconer. "I'm sorry, New Guy. I just...I'm sorry, okay."

"The name's Grandpa," replied Falconer, checking his own pistol, "and forget it. It's fine. I don't want to go in there, neither, but here we are, right?"

Falconer handed his rifle to Walton, and looked up at the big man. "You ever been into a VC tunnel before?"

Walton nodded. "Twice. Don't care to try for a third."

Falconer adjusted his boots and belt. "Any tips? Help a new guy out?"

"Listen more than you look, and trust your gut. You can't see shit in there without turning your torch on, and turning your torch on just tells anyone inside where to shoot."

"What about trusting your gut?"

"I dunno, man. Just do. Maybe your senses can pick up on something your brain can't quite translate, and that's when it comes across as a gut feeling. Just because you can't put a name to it doesn't mean that it's not real."

"That sounds like something Winters would say."

"Yeah, I think he explained it to me like that. Just go easy and be careful, and you'll come back out."

"Right. Any advice for dealing with Bradley?"

"Yeah. If he bites it, check his pockets for weed before you come back out."

CHAPTER TEN

Bradley went first into the tunnel, so hunched over that he was practically waddling, barely able to shift his knees up and down to walk along.

"Would it be better to crawl?" Falconer whispered, behind him.

He felt like Bradley had shrugged, but it was too dark to say for sure.

"It might," came the whispered reply. "Easier to move, but almost impossible to fight back."

"We get in a fight here, we're fucked anyway."

The smell was - in some ways - worse than the darkness. The heavy rainfall of yesterday evening had saturated the soil, even down in the tunnel, which had to be at least ten feet below the crest of the ridge. The smell of the damp earth, combined with a complete lack of ventilation created a humid fug of dirt and decay. The two of them were sweating already, and Falconer could already feel the ache of fatigue in his calves and lower back. There was another scent, too. An acidic tang on top of the dull cloy of the rain.

"You smell that?" Falconer hissed, bumping his head for the tenth time. "Smells kind of acid. What is that?"

Bradley snorted a laugh. "You don't really think they have plumbing in here, do you?"

"Fuck."

"You got that right."

Falconer wiped sweat from his forehead, his elbow hitting the side of the tunnel as he did so. There was barely enough room to do anything besides crawl and sweat. He peered forward into the darkness. It wasn't as totally black as he had initially expected it to be. He could make out some details as he crawled along: an errant root protruding from the tunnel wall, the flex and ripple of Bradley's shirt in front of him. "There's a light source," he whispered. "Kinda orange."

"Yeah, I noticed that, too," Bradley replied, quietly. "The tunnel bends to the left just up ahead. I think that's where the light is coming from."

Falconer nodded reflexively, though there was no way that Bradley could see him. He tried to listen harder, straining for any sounds of movement coming from the tunnel ahead of them. There was the occasional drip of water, but it was echoing so much that he couldn't even begin to guess how far away it was. It could be six feet behind them, or a hundred miles ahead.

It seemed like an hour or more before they reached the bend in the tunnel that Bradley had spotted. They followed it, and discovered that it only went on for another twelve feet or so before leading into a hollowed chamber. The chamber was still roughly hewn, but was massive - easily forty feet long by twenty feet wide, and tall enough for them to able to stand upright in.

"What the hell is this?" Bradley whispered, as he stepped into the chamber, looking around him with his hands on his pistol.

The source of the light was a battery powered lamp resting on a flat, knee-high stone in the centre of the cavern. When it was fully charged, no doubt it would have illuminated the whole room in a bright, white light; but as it was now, it just made everything glow dully orange, strengthening the shadows rather than banishing them.

The more Falconer looked around, the easier it became to pick details out of the blackness. Makeshift bunks were pushed up against the walls, apparently little more than rice matting and some think blankets. The damp soil underfoot still squished, and he for one wouldn't have wanted to sleep down here, with nothing between his sleeping body and the earthworms and slugs. Some rice bowls and a bundle of clothes lay at the foot of each of the bunks.

Bradley looked around. "Four, no, five bunks. Looks like a hidden outpost."

"Could five guys have taken care of all of Hai Trang?"

Bradley shrugged. "Maybe. The farmers weren't exactly well armed."

They slowly advanced, and Falconer felt his boot connect with something hard on the floor. He bent down and felt around. Wood. Smooth, large and heavy. He picked it up and examined it in the feeble light. "AK-47."

"Well, that fucking clinches it. Charlie."

"There was any fucking doubt? Nathaniel Victor doesn't dig tunnels."

"Don't lecture me, New Guy."

They froze suddenly, and Falconer felt his skin crawl.

They had both heard a noise from the other end of the chamber, away in the darkness.

"The fuck was that?" whispered Falconer.

Bradley couldn't see any more in the blackness than he could. "I dunno. Could've been anything."

"Do we risk the torches?"

"Like fuck, man. Advance slowly, weapons up."

"There it is again."

It was a strange sound. Familiar, yet totally incongruous with their surroundings. It was a strange, rushing, tapping noise. Sibilant, yet percussive. It sounded random yet constant, hard yet fluid, like a bag of gravel being emptied. "Rocks? It could be a cave in," he whispered urgently to Bradley.

Bradley didn't answer.

At last, they reached the other side of the chamber. The wall there was bare, except for another tunnel dug into it. Small than the entranceway, this opening was only about three feet wide, and set - somewhat strangely - four feet above the floor of the cavern.

"Why would they put the connecting tunnel so high?" asked Falconer.

"To avoid flooding maybe?" whispered Bradley.

Falconer stepped forward to examine the tunnel more closely. His foot sunk into an ankle high pile of damp soil directly below the opening. "Why would they just leave this earth here?"

"What do you mean?"

"Look at the size of this…Jesus, 'barracks', I guess. They excavated all of this soil, and dumped it up top somewhere. It must have been a big job, but they did it properly. So, why for this tunnel did they just leave the earth dumped here, right where they slept?"

"Maybe they got lazy?"

"No way. Charlie's many things, but he's not lazy."

The rattling, writhing sound was heard again, and this time there was no mistaking its source.

It was coming from the tunnel directly in front of them.

***

"Sergeant, the girl doesn't know anything. I don't know how many other ways there are of asking her the same questions."

Reese flung his cigarette butt down to the ground and stamped it out. "I refuse to believe that the whole village was wiped out by an animal attack. There's no goddamn animal that attacks like that."

Winters shrugged, and not for the first time since the interrogation of Lai Anh had begun. "It's hard to believe, sarge, but to Lai Anh, it *is* the truth. If the Viet Cong came and took her village - as we suspect - then she's mentally blacked it out and replaced Charlie with this animal or monster or demon called the Việt Nam Đen-"

"Yes, Việt Nam Đen…" interrupted Lai Anh. They all turned to look at her.

"You speak English?" Winters asked.

"A little. I try."

"Well, that should speed things up a little bit," said Hanson. "Those Viet Cong that shot at us. You ever seen or heard from them before?"

"No."

"You never had Viet Cong at Hai Trang?"

"Hai Trang, no. They think we have nothing."

Winters was studying the girl. "Why didn't you tell us that you spoke English?"

"Your Vietnamese better than my English." She smiled, shyly.

Reese gestured to Hanson that he wanted a brief conversation with him alone. Winters understood instantly and took Lai Anh by the arm and sat her on a fallen tree, offering her some of his rations.

Reese looked around the area, and sighed. "None of this makes sense."

Hanson took off his helmet and ran his fingers through his hair, attempting to shuck some of the sweat from it. "I've been saying that since I got in country, sarge."

"A village that houses a US spy is attacked and destroyed. Everyone dead or left for dead, signs of small arms fire everywhere. Less than an hour's walk down the trail we find a Viet Cong tunnel system, and some dead Viet Cong."

"Right."

"So, if the Viet Cong didn't attack the village, who did? And if they did, who the hell killed them all when they got back here?"

"You're forgetting something, sarge." Hanson slapped his helmet back on his head. He knew it was risky taking it off for even a second, but sometimes the heat and weight just got too much for him to bear.

"And what is that?"

"The bodies. All desiccated. Sucked dry. Mummified."

"I hate this fucking place," muttered Reese. "As soon as Bradley and Grandpa are out of that fucking rat's nest, we're going full speed back home. No stopping unless we absolutely have to."

"Fucking A, sarge."

***

"Could it be a cave in?" asked Falconer, unable to oust the mental image of being buried alive down in the tunnels. Hurriedly wiping sweat from his brow, he tugged at Bradley's shirt sleeve. "Sounds like it could be a cave in."

Bradley slowly extended an arm into the opening. Falconer couldn't believe that the man was being so bold, and snapped his pistol up to provide what little covering fire he could, lest some insane VC trooper suddenly jumped up from the loose earth, swinging a machete.

Falconer blinked. The pale amber light of the fading lamp had dulled in the time that they had been in there, and was now a reddish brown, barely highlighting anything in the blackness. "Bradley, the lamp's dying. We gotta get out of here."

"The soil's really loose," Bradley said, in the near-darkness, seeming not to have heard him. "This was dug recently. Past few days, maybe. The earth in this chamber has settled; compacted a little. It's been like this a few weeks. This tunnel is new."

"Bradley, man. The light's going. We gotta get out of here, man."

"You got a torch, man."

"We can't fucking turn it on, man! If there's any gooks in there it'll light us up like a fucking Christmas tree!"

"Will you chill the fuck out, man?" Bradley hissed. "You keep yabbering like that and you ain't gonna need to switch the fucking lights on for Charlie to find you, all right?"

"Shut up! Listen...There it is again!"

The rolling and tumbling noise sounded like a hundred feet marching down a gravel pathway, accompanied the slithering, chafing sound of something barrelling down a corridor that was just a touch too small for it. Bradley half-turned in the direction of the tunnel, and barely had time to gasp before a black mass burst forth into him.

Falconer saw something pale brown in the failing light, yet also oddly reflective, glistening like wet leather. He let out a cry of surprise, and snapped his M1911 up, squeezing off two rounds instinctively.

The bright white of the muzzle flash was jarring in that subterranean darkness, burning his retinas into pulsing red, yellow and orange. In those microseconds he first saw the colossal, snake-like creature writhing atop the fallen, shouting Bradley. The second flash - now fired far too wide, he knew - illuminated Bradley, still screaming, blood running down his face as...whatever that thing was...crushed him like an armour plated boa constrictor.

Then, the light of the lamp died completely.

Falconer screamed in pure terror and scurried backwards as fast as he could. His ankles collided with something hard, and he fell backwards, feeling the soft earth give beneath him. Bradley was still screaming, begging for help from man or god - whoever would listen. Falconer screamed with him, involuntarily. The monster in the pitch blackness let out another rattling hiss, and Bradley's screams shot up half an octave.

Falconer felt beneath him, and his hand came into contact with the AK-47 he'd stumbled on earlier. He snatched it up, cocked it and, still laying on the floor, pulled the wooden stock up to his shoulder.

Bradley had stopped screaming.

The noises that were left behind were somehow worse. There was a cracking, and a wet, sighing sound. A rending and a subtle tearing.

Falconer's eyes were wide open, stretching painfully in a desperate search for a single particle of light; but there was none to be had in that underground nightmare. He didn't know what it was that had killed Bradley, but it had looked like a snake of some kind. Did they have anacondas in Vietnam? He didn't know. He didn't think to ask Winters earlier in the day. Winters would have known.

He tried to control his breathing and began slowly crawling backwards, feeling the heels of his boots sink into the damp soil. He had wondered what could have been worse than being barracked in this dungeon, and now he had an answer.

He was confident that the entrance to the chamber, and therefore the tunnel leading into it, had been directly behind them. Yes, they had just walked straight across the chamber, hadn't they?

It sounded as through the snake monster was still feeding on Bradley. The sound of splitting of bone and sinew certainly hadn't moved from that spot. If Falconer was careful, he may be able to make it back to the entry way without disturbing it or alerting it to his presence.

The darkness was all pervading. It wasn't like walking on a moonless night, or even fumbling his way to his bed back in his house back home. There, even in the "darkness" there was always just a touch of ambient light. You might have thought it was dark, but the light still found a thousand ways of leaking in. Your eyes couldn't see much, but they could see outlines, and hints of movement.

Here, there was nothing. There was no difference to him whether his eyes were open or closed. It was worse than being blindfolded.

The creature hissed in the darkness, and there was a wet, splintering sound as another part of Bradley's body gave way to its probing. Satisfied that the creature was distracted, for the time being at least, Falconer began crawling back and away faster, sacrificing stealth for speed, hoping that he could be back out in daylight (or at least out of the chamber and into the main tunnel) before the creature finished eating.

He was making good, silent progress, until the palm of his hand made contact with a discarded bowl of damp, cold rice.

He let out a yelp, a dull cough of disgust and surprise, and hurriedly wiped his hand on his combat pants.

The thing in the darkness fell silent, and he knew he had fucked up.

CHAPTER ELEVEN

A rattling, pulsing breath sounded in the darkness; a gaseous rasp of inquiry. Falconer held his own breathing, desperate to avoid making a single sound that would alert the snake monster to his presence.

After thirty seconds or so his chest began to ache, and he forced himself to breathe in and out at a painfully slow rate. He only allowed himself to breathe a little easier when he saw spots of light in the corner of his vision, and when he heard the wet, peeling noises of the creature feeding on Bradley once more.

Once he was sure that the monster was fully engrossed in its catch, he forced himself to his feet, turned, and began walking slowly back in the direction of the tunnel. Or, at least, the direction he was hopeful that the tunnel was. A flood of cold fear ran through him as he wondered what would happen if he'd become totally disoriented in the pitch blackness, and was actually heading back towards the monster in the darkness. He forced the thought from his mind, and slowly continued walking, a Creedence Clearwater Revival song playing in his head, to distract himself from the noises behind him.

He had to stop himself from gasping when he walked into the wall. His knee was the first to make contact, causing him to stumble a little. He felt a thrill of excitement. He had successfully made it all the way across the chamber, and he'd be back in the daylight before he knew it. An easy trip. Once he found the "doorway" he'd turn back right and before long he'd see light. His eyes would be working again.

But was the doorway to the left or the right of his current position? Where exactly on the wall was he in relation to the entrance?

He didn't know.

He felt a frustrated sob build up in his throat and had to clench his teeth to prevent himself from vocalising it.

A sound in the darkness caused him to freeze.

A new sound.

It wasn't the mashing and rending of the jaws of the monster feeding on Bradley. It was a noise which caused his arm hairs to stand, and a whimper of fear to tremble in his throat.

It was a whispered call, breathy and desperate.

"Grandpa…help."

Bradley was still alive!

Surely that couldn't be? He'd seen blood, he'd heard screams. He was sure he'd seen the creature physically feeding on him.

If he were alive, what sort of condition could he possibly be in?

"Help…me…"

He had to go back and help him, right? "No man left behind" was the credo, wasn't it?

Bradley made an odd, whimpering noise in the darkness and the monster answered with a slither and a rasp of its own.

Falconer knew that he had to try and rescue his injured colleague. Bradley was a dick - there was no getting away from that - but he didn't deserve to die down here, in the darkness with that…thing; and certainly not if Falconer had the chance to do something about it.

Of course, he couldn't just fire indiscriminately into the darkness. He'd be just as likely to hit Bradley as to hit the strange animal that had attacked him. He swallowed. The time for fear was over. He had to see what he was dealing with.

He reached into the side pocket of his combats and pulled out an illumination flare. Once activated, the flare would burn brightly with a reddish light for about four minutes. Plenty of time for him to draw a bead, kill the creature (or at least frighten it off), and run to rescue Bradley…assuming the private was in a rescuable condition.

He popped the cap from the flare and struck it. His vision - now used to the pitch darkness of the cavern - was dazzled by the sudden red-white brightness of the flare. He threw it as far towards the creature and the opposite side of the underground barracks as he could reach. The flare spun and tumbled, bouncing once or twice before coming to a complete stop.

The red tinged glare lit up a sight that made Falconer scream.

Purely by accident, rather than by design, the signal flare had landed right by Bradley's head. The private's eyes were rolled back in his head, and his lips were moving soundlessly, as blood spilled gently onto the floor.

From the chin down, Bradley was invisible. Just that bloodstained face in the red light remained. Obscuring his body and limbs were muscled coils of what Falconer first thought must be some sort of colossal snake, until he saw the many foul, hooked legs sticking from the segmented trunk of the creature. Instantly he was reminded of the event a few days previously when Walton had plucked the centipede from his shoulder.

Distracted by the sudden light and heat of the flare, the creature raised its head and Falconer yelled again, primal terror cracking his voice.

The spurting magnesium flare made the shadows dance manically, and made the giant centipede seem even more monstrous that it would have appeared even in broad daylight. Two long antennae flexed in the air, attempting to process the new signals that its senses were throwing into its primitive brain. Massive mandibles flexed, flicking small particles of meat and blood into the air. The thing's chittering noise set Falconer's teeth on edge.

His primeval, lizard brain kicked into gear and he pulled the Viet Cong AK-47 to his shoulder, firing a semi-automatic burst. He cursed as his rounds struck the ground around the horrendous thing. He pulled a little higher and to the right, hoping to strike the thing dead in the centre of its foul head, when the clip fell empty with a click.

Of course there were only ten bullets left in the goddamn thing. Luck hadn't run his way since he had arrived in country, so why the hell would it want to change now?

He threw the assault rifle to the ground, and snatched the M1911 sidearm from his belt. He saw the creature arc back and begin to scurry to the left and towards him, moving surprisingly fast for such a large, ungainly looking animal.

Then, the flare burned out.

In the wake of the signal flare, the darkness seemed even blacker this time.

The noise of the approaching centipede grew closer and closer.

He acted unthinkingly, and turned and ran into the darkness. He swore and sobbed as he ran straight into the wall. He didn't know where the tunnel was.

The rattling, hissing sound of the centipede, drawing ever closer, had him on the verge of tears. When he'd signed up to fight, he knew that there was every chance he'd end up dying in some far flung corner of the globe, but he'd never *actually* thought that it would happen. He'd always just assumed that he'd be one of the lucky ones who came home and became the grandparent with all the best war stories to tell the young kids, just like his dad had told him about his part in the D-Day landings. In those moments where he had contemplated his own death, he'd always pictured himself dying heroically, in a John Wayne blaze of glory. He'd never imagined dying alone, in the darkness, food for the bugs.

He yanked another flare from his pocket, suppressing a sob as it caught on the material of his combats, finally freeing it and snapping the cap off, striking it fast.

The centipede was only five yards away from him, and its front segments were rearing up to strike. At the sudden glare from the burning magnesium, it hesitated, antenna flailing wildly.

It doesn't like fire... Falconer thought to himself. He remembered something about how all animals naturally feared and avoided fire. Obviously it didn't matter how big they grew...

He held the flare up high, trembling a little, hoping that his little ward would last. The centipede watched him, foul pincers swinging open and closed slowly. He risked a quick glance behind him and spotted the entry way to the tunnel, only ten yards away. He began stepping back towards it, slowly, now focusing once again on the beast.

With each step he took, the creature eased closer, its black body rippling and sliding like plate mail. The antenna seemed drawn magnetically in his direction.

He knew he had to get out of the tunnels. If the AK-47 had simply glanced off of its armour, then his sidearm wouldn't do a thing, either. If he could draw it back out into daylight - he'd never take daylight for granted ever again - then the rest of the squad could provide back up. Walton's M60 ought to make light work of it. Turner had that M79 grenade launcher, too. They'd be drinking and laughing over a pile of pulped bug guts any second now.

He had reached the exit tunnel. He stepped backwards into it, dropping the already fading flare to the ground at the opening, turned, and ran down the tunnel as fast as he could.

The height of the tunnel didn't make it easy. If anything, it seemed smaller than it had when he and Bradley had come this way not ten minutes earlier. His thighs cramped within seconds, and he was forced into a squatting jog, his back hunched over and aching with pain.

He quickened his pace when he heard the thing behind him stirring once more. The flare must have burned out. They were supposed to have a burning time of at least four minutes, but they never did. Like everything else they had it was sub-fucking-par. It was lighter than it had been. The tunnel entrance had to be getting nearer. He began shuffling along as fast as he was physically able.

As he went, he reached into his pocket for his final flare. He had it out of his pocket and had just yanked the cap off when the toe of his boot connected with an errant stone or piece of root and made him stumble. He managed to keep upright, and even keep "running" along, but the flare dropped from his fingers and out of sight. He yelled wordlessly in anger and frustration and fear. The hissing, undulating sound replied back from the darkness, and he knew that he had fucked up. Again.

The tunnel entrance was ahead of him now, no more than thirty yards away. He yelled out for help, knowing that there was every chance he'd never reach them, when he felt the thing's antenna tickle his back. He desperately squeezed his pistol around behind him, muscle cramp in his shoulder making him grit his teeth. He fired off three rounds and the thing backed off. He knew he likely hadn't hurt it, but maybe the light had blinded it, or at least startled it and given it pause for thought.

Ten yards to go. He shouted wordless noises and prayed that he'd make it out of there. If he could just get out of the darkness, he'd have all of his friends there. They'd fight together, and he wouldn't have to die alone in this fucking gook tunnel, torn slowly apart by something shat out of his nightmares.

He didn't remember travelling the last five yards or so. The next thing he knew he was out in the daylight, screaming. The light was painfully bright, and he knew that there was something he had to warn then about. Something he meant to tell them.

Hanson looked Private Falconer up and down. "What the hell happened in there, Falconer? Where's Bradley? You look like you've been through fucking…"

Falconer then remembered what he was supposed to say. "Fucking bug! There's a giant fucking bug in there!"

The centipede spat forth from the tunnel entrance behind him, and reared up in a threatening display of size and power. Hanson dropped his rifle in shock. The rest of the team gasped and swore. Lai Anh screamed and ran into the trees, yelling something unintelligible.

The centipede, shining a brilliant black in the Vietnam sun, lashed forward, its head slamming into Falconer's back. The mandibles crashed forward like a bear trap. He spat up two mouthfuls of blood, and shuddered in a silent scream. The creature reared above them, lifting Falconer ten feet into the air.

"Jesus fucking Christ!" yelled Sergeant Reese.

Winters snapped up his M16 and squeezed off a few rounds. The centipede thrashed back and forth, throwing off his aim. Two pairs of front legs gripped Falconer and he shivered again as a foul neurotoxin was delivered.

The mandibles crunched down again and he screamed, coughing up another pint of blood and bile. The centipede let out a hydraulic sounding hiss, and reversed back into the tunnel as fast as it had come, taking Falconer with it.

"Fall back!" Reese yelled, running into the forest after Lai Anh. Winters, Walton, Turner and Hanson split off in separate directions, running off into the jungle alone.

Hanson's heart was a staccato blast in his chest. It had been a monster. An honest to god monster, straight out of one of the movies he'd snuck into back when he was a kid. He'd loved them back then, when even as a small kid he'd known that they were just stories that couldn't hurt him…but this was different. He's just seen someone lifted into the air and killed by…by what?

He'd run into the trees alone. That was stupid. That was goddamn fucking stupid.

He could hear the others calling. They'd obviously all broken, panicked and ran just like he had. Highly trained soldiers had gone running and screaming because of a bug.

He could hear Turner calling, and it didn't seem too far away. He thought he heard Walton's voice on the breeze, too.

**

It took just over an hour for them to all find each other, and by then the sun was beginning to sink in the sky. Winters claimed he hadn't been scared, and had just run after Lai Anh, knowing that they needed her and she needed them. If it had been anyone else who had claimed that, then the rest of the squad would have mocked them relentlessly, completely disbelieving of their story. For Winters, though, it seemed plausible. The man was robotic at the best of times, and downright cold and detached at the worst. If anyone was going to be completely unshaken by the thing they had seen, it would be Winters.

Turner was the first to raise the question aloud. "What the fuck was that thing?"

It was Lai Anh who answered, her meek, broken voice sounding powerful in the uneasy silence. "Việt Nam Đen."

"And what the fuck does that mean?"

Hanson exchanged a look with Winters before replying. "The Vietnam Black."

CHAPTER TWELVE

Darkness fell quickly in Vietnam. The dense foliage and high trees meant that it got dark long before the sun actually sunk below the horizon, making the shadow rise and colour fade before your eyes. They had set up a camp relatively quickly, and Walton and Winters were already heating up some rations over a small fire.

Turner was quiet, and detached. He had taken himself off to the edge of the campsite, and was sat on large rock, rifle between his legs, staring out into the darkness of the forest. The M79 grenade launcher was with his pack and supplies, nearer to the fire. He rested his chin in his hands, deep in thought.

Corporal Hanson took it upon himself to approach the tall man. "Turner, you okay?"

"We need to go back for him."

Hanson suppressed a wince, turning it into a sigh. "Turner, you know we can't do that. That thing…"

"We go back there and we fucking kill it."

"Look, Grandpa's dead. You know that. You saw it."

"Yeah. I saw it. That's the point. I saw that thing chomp him up real good, and I saw him fucking poisoned or whatever, and I saw him dragged back into that fucking hole. That fucking new guy is dead. So what? New guys get dead. Bradley isn't a fucking new guy. We go back for him."

"No."

Turner rubbed his eyes with the balls of his hands. "We don't know that that thing got him. How do we know he ain't holed up in the tunnel somewhere, hiding from that goddamn thing, and waiting for us to come rescue him? We gotta go back, man."

Hanson sat next to him on the rock. "I want to believe what you're saying. You know I do; but do you even really believe that yourself?"

"I...No. I guess not, but what if I *am* right? We can't fucking leave him behind."

"Look, man, I'll talk to the sarge, but I don't think he's gonna buy it. He just wants us out of here. He wants us back at the base as soon as possible."

"We got two men down, we got a hostage, so why don't we call in a goddamn chopper to get us out of this mess?"

Hanson gestured at the treetops around them. "Where the fuck is it gonna land, Turner? Look, I'll talk to the sarge *and* I'll talk to Walton, maybe see if we can get to an LZ faster than we can get to where we need to on foot."

Turner nodded, his anger subsiding. It was hard to stay angry when a guy like Hanson was being so accommodating. "If you guys are so sure Bradley is dead, then why ain't you calling in a goddamn air strike on that thing?"

"Believe me, if I could, I'd call in a goddamn B-52 on that thing, but I can't see that firing order being taken too seriously, can you? 'Hey, yeah, we got a giant fucking centipede, here. Can you napalm it, pretty please?'"

Turner chuckled at that. "Goddamn you, Hanson."

"I'm sorry about Bradley, I really am. He was a dick, but he was our dick."

"You get that on a greeting card?"

"Wish that you could, Turner. Wish that you could."

They ate an insipid meal of reheated rations. As a kid, Hanson had always been convinced that the slop they served for lunch at school had to be the worst food imaginable. The military, as in so many ways, had widened his experiences on that front. The crap they doled out at training camp was worse, the crap at the front line base worse than that, and then finally there were the freeze dried rations you took out on patrol with you. The emphasis was in pumping you full of enough calories and vitamins to keep you alive in the short term, not flavour or texture.

Lai Anh was visibly disgusted, but the rest of them were all used to it by now.

Hanson was the first on watch. The flickering orange of the fire made it difficult to watch the perimeter. Not only did it make shadows move and dance, hiding any potential enemy movement, but it also affected his night vision. His eyes were never truly able to adjust to the dark, or the light. When his stint was over, it was Winters' turn, and the rest of them turned in for the night, determined to get some sleep before the next long march.

Lai Anh sat with Winters, watching the forest with him. "What do we look for?" she whispered.

"Movement. Anything that isn't immediately obviously the wind is cause for concern and should be watched. Any flash; it could be moonlight on a bayonet or a barrel. Any noise. Anything unusual."

"What made you come to Vietnam?"

Winters shrugged, and whispered back, "I was sent here by my country. There was no arguing with it."

"I mean, why did you join up?"

"I didn't have a lot of choice. School thought I was dumb, every business in town thought I was weird and wouldn't give me a job, so I went into the military. I figured that if I didn't enjoy it, I could at least use the time to learn things."

Lai Anh nodded, and sat quietly. At the end of Winters' shift, Turner clapped a hand on his shoulder. "My turn, little man."

Winters stood, nodded, and guided the half-asleep Lai Anh back to where everyone was sleeping.

Turner watched them head off, and counted off six hundred seconds. By then, he was certain that pretty much everyone was asleep. Everyone in the military learnt hard and fast that you took your chances to sleep whenever you could, because you didn't know when the next chance was going to come along. So, he was certain that everyone else had been out before he'd approached Winters, and he was pretty sure he'd be out already. The girl was no concern either. She'd been practically asleep on her feet the whole time.

He slung the M79 grenade launcher across his shoulder, and held his M16 assault rifle in his hands. He knew that what he was about to do was potentially a suicide mission and, at best, a court martial for leaving his post. He didn't care. He knew that there had to be a chance that Bradley was still alive, and if he was, he was going back for him. He eased himself to his feet, slowly, and tiptoed around the perimeter of the camp site.

He trod slowly and carefully, not even wanting to crack a twig, fearful of waking the sergeant - or any of them, for that matter.

He reached the edge of the trees, and began walking back the way they had come. The journey was even harder by nightfall, as his eyes constantly flickered from side to side, fearing a sudden Viet Cong ambush as much as he feared running into the centipede again. The calls and scurries of the indigenous wildlife of Vietnam didn't do anything to allay his paranoia. Even after nine months in country, Vietnam might as well have been an alien world.

He slapped away insects and - on one occasion - had to forcibly kick a snake from his path. It was as though all the animals of the jungle objected to his presence there. The country didn't want the war any more than the innocent people caught in the crossfire did.

Turner pushed these strange thoughts from his mind, and went deeper into the jungle.

***

"Where the fuck is he?"

Sergeant Reese had Winters held firmly by the scruff of his shirt, and was shouting loudly an inch from his face.

"I don't know, sarge!"

"You were the last one to see him. Where the fuck was he?"

The sergeant let go suddenly and Winters fell to the floor on his backside. "I don't know, sarge. He relieved me from watch, and took over my spot. Then I went to sleep. I didn't see him after that."

"And none of you other motherfuckers heard anything? Turner just gets fucking ghosted ten feet from where we're sleeping? Not one of us wakes up? I don't buy that for a motherfucking *second*."

A cold chill ran through Hanson. "Sarge, I think I know where he's gone."

"Oh, you do, Hanson? Well, how about you share what's so funny with the rest of the fucking class?"

Hanson rubbed his eyes in exasperation. "He's gone back for Bradley."

Reese was stunned for a moment, before his next outburst. "What do you mean 'he's gone back for Bradley'? Bradley's fucking dead, back in the tunnels with that fucking thing that ate the FNG. What the fuck is Turner gonna do, Hanson?"

"He doesn't believe he's dead. He told me so yesterday. He wanted us all to go back and look for him. I told him I'd talk to you in the morning, but obviously he decided he didn't want to wait to see what you had to say. He's gone back to the tunnels."

"Fuck!" Reese yelled at the sky.

Hanson lit a cigarette and waited patiently while the sarge spat and swore his anger out. Eventually, his rage abated and he became more lucid. "Well, what the fuck do we do now? We got two dead, one deserted; leaving us with four guys and one gook bitch. We've got another two days march, easy, and probably Charlie the whole fucking way knowing our rotten luck so far. Oh, yeah, and there's a goddamn fucking monster caterpillar motherfucker out there. What the fuck do we do now, Corporal?"

"We go looking for Turner."

"What did you say, motherfucker?"

"We go looking for Turner. We need him. For all we know, he only left a half hour ago, and we could catch him easy. Also, he's got the goddamned grenade launcher, and if we *are* going to get attacked by giant bugs and Viet Cong and who knows what else, I want a grenade launcher."

"Fine. You know what, Winters and I will stay here, and we'll pack up all this shit, and we'll plan our route back home. You and Walton can go look for Turner."

"Me?" Walton whined. "What the fuck did I do wrong?"

"Shut your big ass up, Walton, and get with the Corporal. Hanson, back here in half an hour. No longer."

"Yes, sarge."

***

"Shit, man, I've never seen the sarge like this before," muttered Walton as they made their way through the jungle. "Have you?"

"Yeah, once. He nearly fell out of a chopper."

"He was so angry he nearly fell out of a chopper?"

Hanson laughed. "No, he nearly fell out of the side door of a Huey, and everyone laughed at him. That made him mad as hell."

"Jesus. How high up were you?"

"We hadn't taken off yet."

Walton chuckled, picturing the sarge stumbling a few feet to the floor to the raucous laughter of the squad. "The maddest I ever saw him was one time when w-"

They had found Turner.

"Jesus..." whispered Hanson. "Son of a bitch didn't even make it three hundred yards."

"Did he get shot in the ass?" asked Walton, incredulously.

The dead man lay face down in the undergrowth, feet pointing towards them. Blood saturated his combats across his ass-cheeks, and down his thighs.

They approached slowly. Hanson kept his rifle trained on Turner's body, watching the ground. Walton swung his M60 in a wide arc from left to right, watching the trees.

"Fuck me..." whispered Hanson, as they got closer.

It was no gunshot wound. Turner's groin and upper legs were in tatters. Shredded flaps of skin and cloth were still wet with glistening red blood.

"Claymore?" asked Walton, glancing back at the trees.

"No way. Not unless it went off while he had one leg either side of it. Besides, we'd have heard it. Those things go off like a shotgun blast."

Hanson knelt by the body, studied it momentarily, and then spontaneously vomited. "He's...fucking been chewed out. Didn't Winters say something about some animal he'd found being 'cored'?"

Walton shrugged, still keeping lookout. "I dunno, man. Winters says lots of things, and I'm damned if I understand even half of them."

"It's all been chewed off down there, anyway. You think there'd be more blood, but…I dunno, maybe it soaked into the ground or something."

He wiped vomit from his chin, and then pressed down on Turner's stomach. "He's been gutted. It's like there's nothing in there. That thing…the centipede…it must have just…eaten his insides. It's exactly what it did to the animal Winters found."

"This is fucking grotesque, man."

"Don't you get it? All those desiccated bodies we found? They weren't desiccated. They'd been hollowed out by that fucking thing. That's how it feeds."

"You serious?"

"It's gotta be, Winters. Doesn't it all add up? I mean, that's how spiders feed, isn't it? They catch a fly and they eat all the insides, leaving a shell that they just throw away? Maybe centipedes do the same thing!"

He rolled Turner over onto his back. He let out a gasp and fell back at the expression on the dead man's face. The eyes were wide, bulging, and partially rolled back. His mouth was pulled downward in a grimace of extreme pain, the tongue fallen back into the throat. A dribble of blood had run down his chin and cheek, and was now partially dried, still sticky. "It's gotta be venomous. The other centipedes are, right?"

"That's what they say. Never been stupid enough to be bitten by one. I remember back at the base, some of the guys used to do bug fights. They'd make a little arena and you'd place bets on centipedes, scorpions, tarantulas…whatever they could find. It was never my thing, but one of the guys died when one of the tarantulas bit him. Stupid fucking way to die. Fly out to a war zone and get killed because you're fucking with the wildlife."

"Falconer…New Guy…Grandpa. He was shivering and shaking when it got him. That's got to be some toxin." He steeled himself, reached to Turner's neck, and snapped off a dog tag.

Walton tapped him on the shoulder. "I'm hearing 'there's a giant fucking centipede that eats your fucking insides', so what the fuck are we still doing here, man?"

Hanson got slowly to his feet, wiping his blood and vomit stained hands on his pants, and grabbed the fallen grenade launcher. "You're right. We gotta tell the sarge and we gotta get out of here as fast as we can."

They slowly turned, and quickly walked back to the campsite, leaving the body of Private Robert Turner to the plants and the birds.

And the bugs.

CHAPTER THIRTEEN

The squad took the news of Turner's death much better than Hanson had expected. He guessed that they had been half-expecting it as soon as he and Walton had walked into the jungle to go looking for him. Hanson had certainly been expecting it himself. One man walking into the jungle by himself was asking for trouble.

He hoped it had been quick; or, at least, quicker than the Viet Cong would have made it if they'd been the ones to find him.

The day passed without event, which was a welcome change of pace. The march was a long and boring one, not to mention hot and tiring. The sun had just begun to set, the light turning a dull orange, when they pushed through a line of trees, and onto a much wider path, at least eighteen feet wide.

It must have been regularly used by the locals, first on foot, and then by cart, and eventually by small trucks. It would certainly have been possible to fit a tank down here, but Hanson doubted that anyone had ever tried. The US used tanks more often than the media would have had you suspect, but they were mostly used for fire support in village and urban fighting. There was no true benefit to having one trundling through the jungle, unable to bring its turret to bear on anything. The jungle was for small arms fire and, occasionally, hand to hand. An air strike could be called upon if desperately needed, and there was the possibility of close air support from a chopper, but mostly you were on your own.

They kept walking, determined to get as far as they could before they were forced to bed down for the night.

Sergeant Reese had shifted his pace so that he was walking alongside Corporal Hanson. "Dumb ass motherfucker."

"Huh?"

"Turner."

Hanson sighed. "I should have suspected he was going to do something like that. He and Bradley were really close. I should have kept an eye on him."

"You weren't to know he was going to be that dumb."

"I've been thinking on that," said Winters, who had overheard their conversation. He held the grip of his rifle in one hand, the other on Lai Anh's arm, "and I think he might have actually kept us alive last night."

"How do you mean?" asked Hanson.

"Think about it. That thing must have been out on the patrol for food when it spotted Turner."

"You think that thing was following us?" Sergeant Reese fumbled for a cigarette.

"No, sarge. I think it was just out looking for food. It stumbled across Turner and took him down. Maybe it rushed him, or maybe it lay in wait. I don't know much about how centipedes hunt, I'm afraid. In any event, it found him and ate him. If he hadn't have been there, the Vietnam Black would probably have kept hunting, and may have found our camp. If it had, I think the casualties may have been higher."

"The Việt Nam Đen is a killer," said Lai Anh. "Many beasts hunt while they are hungry. The Việt Nam Đen will kill indiscriminately. It is the foulest tempered of all the monsters of Vietnam."

"All the monsters?" asked Walton, but no-one answered him.

"That night it came to the village, it only came to take a pig. Most of us were still asleep. When we heard the noise the pig made, one of the villagers...I don't know who...ran out to defend it. He must have attacked it; threw a rock, maybe. Then we heard *his* screams. The other villagers ran out to see what was happening. Some had blades. Some had guns. The Việt Nam Đen did not care."

The squad had slowed down to listen to her story.

"I saw my father swing at one of its legs with his knife. It was biting a young girl from the other side of the street, and didn't see him. The blade broke, and the thing didn't care. When it had thrown the broken woman against the side of a building, it turned on him. It turned, and I thought I could see the hate in its demonic eyes. It just…leapt onto him, and curled into a ball around him. I couldn't see him anymore. The thing just consumed him in its blackness, a bundle of legs and armour. I ran, and I never saw him again."

She fell silent at this, and so did the rest of the squad. They gradually picked up their pace once more, continuing down the wide path.

It was some time, perhaps even an hour, before anyone broke the silence. Reese whispered. "Walton, how much further do we stay on this path?"

Walton was on point, swinging his M60 machine gun left and right, keeping watch lest someone - or something - might burst out of the trees. "Some time yet, sarge. This is a long hard slog. At the end, this path leads back into the trees, and then there's supposed to be a pretty big clearing. I figure we could stop there for the night, and then it's another march tomorrow to the river. Then we follow the river nearly all the way home."

"You make it sound so easy."

"It's what I do."

Hanson struck up a conversation with Winters. "So, what is this thing? How does a centipede get this big? Is it just, like, super old or something?"

Winters shrugged. "I don't think that's how invertebrates work. I don't know, though. Some of the underwater ones might just keep getting larger and larger, but that seems impractical for a land creature, doesn't it?"

"Don't ask me, man. You're the brainbox. How do you know all this stuff, anyhow?"

Winters shrugged again. He did that a lot. "I read a lot. I pick stuff up. I remember things. You know how it is."

"Uh-huh. So what are we dealing with here if it isn't just an overgrown bug."

"I'd guess at a new species. Well, new to Western civilisation anyway. The way Lai Anh speaks of it seems to indicate that it's at least well known to the indigenous population. A rare sighting, for sure, but one that's still known of and spoken about."

"This has been a fucked up mission."

"Yes, it has."

Walton was the first to hear the noise. Off in the jungle to the right of the path, he heard branches cracking and being knocked aside. His first instinct was that a car, or something like it, was being rolled towards them with its engine off. He had heard no engine, but the rolling, crackling sensation was very similar. He braced his legs, and swung the large M60 machine gun in the direction of the noise, yelling "Heads up!" to the rest of the squad.

Winters shoved Lai Anh behind him, dropped to one knee and readied his M16. Hanson and Reese stood where they were and snapped their guns up, stocks tight against their shoulders, leaning into it a little to offset the recoil.

The bracken bent back, the bracken cracking, and the Vietnam Black walked onto the path.

The whole squad froze.

If it had been NVA or VC, they'd have cut them dead with a volley of fire, but the colossal centipede didn't seem to have noticed them. It hadn't barged onto the scene and reared up in an attack like it had done with Falconer back at the VC tunnels. It was just...exploring.

Somehow, to Hanson, this actually made it worse. Normally animals were wary of man. Whenever - back when he was a kid - he'd gone hunting with his uncle, he remembered that he'd been told to be super quiet and calm, because the animals knew that they were being hunted, and even the slightest noise to startle them would let them run and get away. "Going to ground" his uncle had called it.

Seeing the creature now made his arm hairs rise. He knew it was because this thing had no natural predators. Nothing. No tarantula or monkey or bird of prey would be able to feed on this armour plated monster.

The entire thing was black. Jet black. So black that the light reflected blue from its surface. The punched in looking head was about three feet across, the wicked, scythe-like mandibles swinging gently. The antenna - also black - flexed and twitched...then stopped as the monster's head moved in their direction.

The Vietnam Black slowly lifted up the first seven or eight segments, so that it towered over them, its head ten feet up in the air. The legs flexed, and Hanson suspected they were just as poisoned tipped and deadly as the mandibles.

Time seemed to slow down as the thing swayed there. Finally it let out a hiss and pulled backwards, ready to strike.

"Open fire!" Reese shouted, yanking hard at the trigger of his M16, throwing his own aim off in a panic. Reese saw the bullets strike the mud in front of it. He aimed high, but it was almost as though the centipede guessed his intentions and threw its head back and forth in an attempt to throw him off. He squeezed off a few rounds, but they had little effect. Winters' bullets joined his own, and he saw them sparking off of the thing's iron hide.

"Get the grenade launcher!" Hanson shouted across to Reese. "Use the goddamn grenade launcher, sarge!"

Reese dropped his gun and fumbled with the grenade launcher, trying to open the breech and load it as fast as he was able.

The Vietnam Black snaked towards the sergeant.

"Winters!" shouted Hanson. "Get a flare. Maybe it hates fire."

Winters hadn't heard him, and just kept up semi-automatic fire from his own weapon. Lai Anh cowered behind him, her hands over her ears, face screwed up in sheer terror.

The centipede let out a piercing screech, and then came the rasping chuka-chuka-chuka noise of Walton's M60 machine gun. The much larger weapon seemed to get the Vietnam Black's attention where the smaller M16 assault rifles had failed. Walton yelled out a wordless challenge to the thing, and advanced foolhardishly towards it, firing off bursts of three to six bullets at a time.

Hanson saw one of the rounds strike a leg at the joint and shear it off. A strange, thick yellow blood pumped out as the limb was amputated. The thing barely seemed to notice. It rushed forward and snapped its mandibles at the sergeant, letting out another obnoxious hiss. Hanson swung his own weapon upward, desperately hoping that he could clip it in the eye, or perhaps shear off one of the antenna. He remembered, vaguely, seeing a movie when he was a kid about giant ants in the New Mexico desert, and that you could kill them by shooting their antennae. This thing was too fast and too well armoured, though, and his bullets had no noticeable effect.

He ducked and rolled as he saw Walton pivot on the spot and plant his back foot before the chuka-chuka-chuka of the M60 deafened him. Some of the rounds seem to graze the armour, but none were able to fully pierce it; at least, not as far as he could see. Another leg took a hit, and was left hanging on by a thread of cartilage.

His own rifle clicked empty, and he watched helpless as the beast turned and surged towards Walton. The big man refused to back down, and dug his heels in, firing as best he could, desperately trying to get the heavy weapon up high enough to get a head shot on the demonic bug.

There was a high pitched scream, and Hanson saw Lai Anh running past him, straight toward the Vietnam Black. She must have grabbed a flare from Winters, and was now holding it high, and waving it from left to right in a high arc in front of Walton. The centipede seemed confused and a little cowed, backing away from the bright magnesium flame.

She yelled at it in incoherent Vietnamese and it hissed shrilly, before turning and charging back into the undergrowth, leaving a trail of foul smelling, thick, yellow blood behind it. Lai Anh, her adrenaline spent, dropped to her knees on the floor, sobbing. The flare burned out and fell from her limp hands. Winters went to her side and she pulled him down to her, burying her face in his chest. The typically stoic private didn't seem to know quite how to react, and contented himself with a gentle "there there" pat on her back, and stayed kneeling with her until she was ready to stand.

Hanson had to wonder if that was the closest he'd ever been to a woman.

The rest of the squad slowly lowered their weapons, and no-one said a word. For a moment, the only sounds were the wind and the quiet whimpering of Lai Anh.

Walton was the first to break the silence. "Well, there's something you don't see every day."

"Our rifles didn't do shit," muttered Sergeant Reese.

"Right," agreed Hanson. "You could just see them bouncing off. Walton did some damage, but he went through more than a few rounds doing it. A lot of bullets for not much in the way of returns."

Walton had picked up one of the legs he had severed, the ichor still dripping down from it like rancid custard.

"Watch it, Walton!" Hanson yelled. "They could be poisonous."

The large man dropped it quickly, wiping his hands on the leg of his pants. "It didn't bother it none, though. Losing a leg, two even, didn't slow it down. Didn't make it think twice. It just kept coming. Fuck, man."

"We need to get to the clearing, and set up camp. Sun's already hit the horizon."

Reese nodded. "Winters, get the girl up and moving. I want us at that clearing inside the hour, and I want us prepared for if this fucking thing comes back for us again."

Winters helped the girl to her feet, although she still clung to him for support.

Hanson was frustrated. "We ain't got much in the way of protection. If the M16s aren't stopping this thing, and Walton's big gun got ignored, what are you hoping we can do?"

Reese shrugged. "We got the grenade launcher. We got claymores."

"Yeah. We got claymores, spit and signal flares."

"Then we make do with what we've got, Corporal. Cut the chatter and let's get up and on the road already."

"Yes, sarge."

CHAPTER FOURTEEN

The sun was halfway below the horizon - or so they guessed, the foliage made it impossible to say for sure - by the time they reached camp. The blue-black dark of night made the entire clearing dangerous. Even putting aside the problem of the giant centipede that hunted them, they were still deep in NVA and Viet Cong territory. Any number of enemy troops and insurgents could be watching them from the tree line and they wouldn't know about it until too late.

The five of them prepared to sleep as near to the centre of the clearing as they could. It made them easier to spot, for sure, but it did also mean that they'd get the most warning in the event that someone - or something - did intrude on the area.

Between them they had four M18 Claymore mines. Resembling something like a lunchbox, and bearing the only-semi-humorous, stencilled instructions "Front Toward Enemy", the Claymores were an excellent anti-personnel weapon, and perfect for sentry duty. Traditionally detonated by remote control, it was also relatively easy to set them up to be triggered by a timer or, as they had this night, by a tripwire.

One Claymore was positioned at the tree line at each cardinal point of the compass, giving them the best coverage and protection against the Vietnam Black and the Viet Cong that they could hope for. When the tripwire was pulled, the small C4 charge inside the plastic casing of the Claymore would explode, sending the payload - several hundred steel ball bearings - rocketing forward like a shotgun blast from hell. If it hit a man, he'd be cut down in a second. If it was a giant, armour plated, poisonous, invertebrate killing machine then, well, they'd have to find out exactly how effective that was when they got there.

Winters pulled first watch, and sat just at the edge of where the rest of them lay down, his M16 ready, the safety deliberately in the off position. He squinted out into the darkness, but knew there was very little chance of him seeing anything. In fact, the harder he looked, the more likely it was that he'd trick himself into seeing something that wasn't there. Trying to spot a black shiny creature moving through the darkness was next to impossible.

Lai Anh lay sleeping, although it had taken a lot of calming down to get her to be this relaxed. Reese and Hanson were sitting upright, backs against their packs, relaxing as much as was physically possible. Walton was curled up in a ball on his side, snoring gently.

Winters lit a cigarette from his pocket. He rarely smoked, and only did so when he felt tired, convincing himself that as nicotine was a stimulant it would work in the same way as a good, old-fashioned pot of coffee. The smoke stung his eyes and he had to rub them roughly as they watered, blurring his vision.

***

He didn't notice the long, rippling black shape moving up in the tree branches, steering clear of the tripwires they had so carefully placed and hidden. Such tricks were not unknown to it. The spiders of the deepest jungles used similar traps to ensnare their prey, and since it was young it had learned that such silken material was to be avoided. It crept up along the trees, occasionally startling a bird or monkey from its sleeping place, and slowly began to stalk around the group.

One of the group was sitting up, obviously keeping watch like it had seen small groups of monkeys do before. One was always there to watch for predators. If one could remove the sentry, then the rest of the group should be easy pickings.

Yes, if it could take that one, then the rest would die quickly, and it could feed at its leisure.

***

Winters flicked the cigarette butt to the ground, rubbed his stinging eyes again and checked his watch. Another twenty minutes to go until he could get some sleep, sending Corporal Hanson up here to keep watch in his place.

A rustling noise sounded from the knee-high grass to his left, and he stood bolt upright, pulling his rifle up to his shoulder.

Too late, of course. The Vietnam Black charged forward, its many legs propelling it at high speed toward him. Winters squeezed off two shots, barking loud and bright in the darkness, before the thing was on him. He let out a scream as the front legs wrapped rapidly around his shoulders, the mandibles crunched down on his skull, and the sheer weight of the nightmarish thing forcing him to the ground.

His shout had woken the others, but by the time they stood, weapons in hand, it was too late. The entire length of the Vietnam Black was curled up around him, the legs injecting their venom, the mandibles pulverising his skull and consuming his brain.

Horrified by the shrieks of abject terror from the normally stoic Winters, Hanson pumped several rounds from his assault rifle into the monster. Seeing it undulate a little, he gained a little satisfaction from the fact that his attack at least bothered the thing at this range. Hearing another wordless whimper from Winters, he tried to get a shot on the fallen soldier instead, at least saving him the fate of being eaten alive that had befallen Turner, Falconer, and the villagers of Hai Trang. It was impossible. The ropy, muscular mass of the Vietnam Black had now completely obscured Winters into a hell of venom, smothering and being eaten alive.

Hanson ducked to the side at the distinctive chuka-chuka-chuka of Walton's M60 machine gun. He saw rounds penetrate the hard chitin at this close range and that yellow bloody ichor pumping out. The monster writhed, and reared its head up, mandibles dripping pink from where it had been feeding on Winters' brain matter.

In the blackness of the night, it made the thing seem even more alien.

"Fall back!" shouted Sergeant Reese, gripping Hanson's arm and tugging him towards the tree line.

"Are you fucking kidding, sarge?" Hanson yelled. "There's nowhere to fall back to! It lives in the fucking jungle!"

He pumped a few more rounds into it, as did Walton. The M60 was designed for suppressive fire and was nowhere near accurate enough for a target this agile. Lai Anh's scream split the night and, in the muzzle flash of the machine gun, he saw her break and run for the jungle.

The thing struck out like a rattlesnake at Walton, and the big man fell back hard on his backside. For a moment, Hanson was sure that the man's time had come, but Walton managed to swing out a boot and crack the thing hard across the head. It didn't seem to hurt it, but it certainly startled and it made it hesitate long enough for him to scramble to his feet.

Inspiration came, and Hanson snatched a flare from his pocket and struck it. He remembered that back on the road an hour or so ago, the thing had ducked sharply away from the bright light of the flare in the growing darkness. He threw it low, and it landed just at Walton's feet. Again, the Vietnam Black ducked away, hissing in frustration at the light and heat of the burning magnesium. Walton fired several more rounds, then turn and ran for the trees.

Again Sergeant Reese tugged at Hanson's arm. "Come on! We've got to go! Split up! We can give it the run around, hole up and find each other again when the sun comes. We've got to go, Corporal!"

Hanson, seeing the pale, waxy face of Winters laying in the coils of the rear half of the centipede, knew that the Sergeant was right. He lifted his rifle one last time, firing a bullet into Winters' forehead, and then turned and ran.

It was only just as they reached the tree line that he realised their mistake.

Winters and Lai Anh had lucked out, but Sergeant Reese was not so fortunate.

As he reached the edge of the tree line, his boot caught in the trip wire of a Claymore.

He managed to run two more steps before the C4 detonated, placing him full in the line of fire. The one-eighth of an inch diameter steel balls shot forth at a speed of nearly four thousand feet per second, each breaking into individual fragments. The blast hit him like a shotgun blast to the stomach, and he fell.

Hanson screamed, and slid to the floor beside him, trying to assess the Sergeant's injuries in the darkness. The lack of light made it hard to see for sure, but it looked as though his shirt and jacket were already saturated with blood.

Dare he strike a flare? It may drive away the Vietnam Black - which was hopefully still occupied with Winters, anyway - but if there were any Viet Cong in the area he'd be lit up like a Christmas Tree.

Sergeant Reese coughed wetly, and Hanson knew that whatever it was, it wasn't good. He fumbled around in the darkness, his hands instantly black with blood.

The medical kit was back at the camp. They'd left everything behind.

They'd just grabbed their weapons and run. The medical supplies, the rations, the radio…everything was back in the clearing. He looked over towards their discarded packs, just visible in the darkness. He could see the hideous Vietnam Black curled up into a ball around the dead Liam Winters, occasionally shifting as the mass of the dead man shrank beneath it.

Could he run back and grab the medical kit? Would it do them any good if he did?

Reese's breathing was becoming a gasp, bubbling slightly. Shallower, more rapid. "Guys, I think I fucked up."

Hanson fumbled around in the darkness, yelping as his hand came into contact with something that wriggled away into the foliage. He'd never look at snakes or bugs the same way again. He'd never really before considered them up close, but magnified as the Vietnam Black was, he realised that monsters were very much alive on the earth.

He finally found what he was looking for: the sarge's fallen helmet. He ripped the syrettes of morphine from the helmet's band and stuck both of them into Reese's arm, squeezing to administer the maximum dosage possible. It was a matter of seconds before Reese's eyes fluttered closed and he breathed a little easier.

He pulled the sergeant's M1911 pistol from his belt and placed it in his hand. "Sarge, you know what this is?"

"Uh-huh."

"I'm going to find Walton, and we're going to get out of here. We know where you are - you're by the clearing on the map, okay? You stay here and just rest, okay? If anyone in a coolie hat comes by, you've got your gun, okay? Anything comes by looking like that motherfucking bug, you've got your gun, okay? And if..." he couldn't finish.

"If the morphine runs out, and it hurts too bad, I've got my gun."

Hanson swallowed. "Yeah."

"I died in a real fucking stupid way didn't I?"

Hanson stifled a sob so that it came out like a laugh. "You want me to tell everyone you went out in a blaze of glory?"

"You can tell the boys what you want. Tell Carrie the truth. Letter's in my inside pocket."

Hanson grabbed the letter to Reese's wife, and stashed it with his own in his jacket pocket. "I will. I'm not going to send that letter, though. We're going to send the chopper back in a day or two, and we'll come get you, okay?"

"Sure. Go get Walton and the girl."

Hanson stood. He looked back to Reese to see if there was anything else that remained to be said, but the sergeant was already dreaming in a morphine induced daze.

He did notice one thing, though.

He slid the M79 grenade launcher from the sleeping Sergeant's shoulder and slung it over his own. If someone did find him, then the grenade launcher would be doing him no favours whatsoever at that range. He, Walton and Lai Anh, however, may well have need of it. Hanson gripped his M16 in both hands and ran in the direction that Walton had headed, calling his name.

He ran straight into Lai Anh. The girl screamed and they both fell to the floor. He saw her instantly try and scramble to her feet once again to run, but he gripped her by the arms and held her down. "Lai Anh! Wait! It's me!"

The girl turned to him, eyes wide as an owl's, sweat and tears and dirt marking her entire face. She gibbered at him in Vietnamese, and he didn't pick out any of it, apart from the phrase 'Việt Nam Đen' again and again. He pressed the palm of his hand to her mouth and her yammering became a mumble. He shushed and whispered comforting words to her until she fell quiet and he saw the panic leaving her eyes.

He removed his hand, and the first word she whispered was "Winters?"

He shook his head slowly. "No."

"It got him?"

He had an instant flash memory of shooting the fallen man in the forehead just moments ago. "Yeah. The centipede got him."

She nodded shakily. "I liked him."

"We all did. He was a great guy. He was smart, he was funny, and he was brave."

"You are sure he is dead?"

He heard the bullet fired. He saw the red blossom and run down his pale face, trapped in the ropey muscle of the Vietnam Black. "I'm sure."

"Your other man. He was not sure they were dead."

"I'm sure Winters is dead."

"How are you sure?"

He didn't want to have to tell her. "I'm sure."

"Where is the other? The one who leads?"

"Reese?"

"Yes. Reese?"

He slowly got to his feet. "He's hurt. I've treated him as best as I could, but we have to leave him for now. Once we can get back home, we can send doctors for him, but I've done all I can for now."

"What if the Việt Nam Đen comes?"

Hanson's jaw clenched. "We hope it doesn't, and we hope that I made the right choice."

"This means that you now lead?"

He nodded. "Looks that way."

She wiped the tears from her eyes and nodded. "What do we do now?"

"We find Walton."

"The large man with the large gun?"

"The large man with the large gun."

It did not take them long to find him. He had known not to run and stray too far. He was waiting by a tree near the clearing, but well out of sight (and hopefully smell) of the centipede. He was so well hidden, in fact, that they didn't notice he was there until they had walked past him, and he had stepped out, clapping a hand on Hanson's shoulder.

"Jesus Christ, what the fuck, Walton?"

"Hey, that was funny."

"Nothing about tonight is fucking funny, man."

PART THREE

RUN THROUGH THE JUNGLE

CHAPTER FIFTEEN

They didn't start the march again until the sun was high in the sky. Hanson's head told him that it was best they got marching as soon as possible, but his heart knew that the three of them needed the daylight to banish the ghosts of the previous night.

He felt bad about making the sergeant wait, but he also knew that there was a good chance he was dead already. The gut shot had been pretty severe; he'd been right by the Claymore when it had detonated. There was every chance he'd bled out already. In any event, another few hours wouldn't make any difference to the - likely already pre-determined - outcome.

Their packs were way behind them, now, and he wasn't sure he'd be able to find his way back to them, even if he wanted to chance both the appearance of the centipede *and* the chance of triggering another of their own Claymores.

He popped open the holster of his M1911 sidearm, checked that it was loaded, reversed the grip and handed it to Lai Anh. "You used one of these before?"

"Rifle. Once."

"Okay." He stood behind her and showed her the proper way to grip the pistol, one hand supporting the wrist of the other. "You don't have to be too accurate, because we're not at the rifle range here. All you need to do is point that thing at whatever's coming for you, and squeeze the trigger. Squeeze it, don't yank on it. You understand me?"

"I understand. Thank you."

"Don't mention it. I don't know that'll it do much to stop that thing, but if we run into...softer targets...it'll help you out."

She nodded, sticking it in the waistband of her pants.

Hanson yanked it out and showed her how to put on the safety.

She nodded, sticking it back in the waistband of her pants.

Walton led the way. The man's innate sense of direction made Hanson wonder if he was part Cherokee or something.

Lai Anh followed behind the two of them, feeling like a true part of the squad now that she had a weapon of her own.

She kept glancing behind them, wondering if there was some way she could convince them to turn around and search for Winters. She missed him already. Corporal Hanson was nice enough, and the other one - Walton, was it? - was also very kind to her. It wasn't so much that she thought Winters was necessarily worthier than the others, but rather that she didn't like the idea of him being left behind.

Her chance came after another half an hour or so, when Walton wanted to stop and check the map against the compass. "I'm pretty sure I know I'm right, but I'm not having this be all my fucking fault if we lose an hour or wind up in a tunnel sucking gook dick for the rest of the war."

Hanson chuckled and sat down at the base of a tree, lit a cigarette and closed his eyes.

Lai Anh knew she would never have another chance, and snuck away, back the way they had come.

She was young, slender and moved quickly through the trees. Even running, she was quieter than the big American men with their armour and weapons.

However, she was a long way from her home of Hai Trang, and it wasn't long before she was lost. A cold chill of fear ran up inside her and she remembered when she had once gotten lost in the jungle as a small child. She had sat down and cried, terrified that she would never see her mother again. Then the rain had come.

It was several hours before her father found her, by which time she was soaked to the skin and shivering. It was only sheer luck that had led her father to her. She had left no trail and made no sound. The relief at being carried back home was tempered by the fear that her mother would be angry at her for running off and beat her, but she had not. Her mother had burst into tears and hugged the life from her, before taking her into their hut and warming her up and cuddling her to sleep.

Now, she had run away from the only people in the jungle she could rely on, and for what? For a man who was most likely dead.

She decided that, as she was completely lost, then any direction was as good as any other, and she struck out in the way she had originally been heading.

It was the noise that made her stop dead in her tracks. The rasping, chittering rattle followed by a wet, mashing sound. There was a dribbling crunch, which reminded her of her fat uncle devouring seafood in the market, legs and crustacean guts running down his chin.

She looked down and saw that her toe was two inches from the glistening hide of the Vietnam Black.

If it hadn't have made that noise when it did, she would have walked straight into it.

All her bravado of just minutes ago, barging off into the wilderness like a warrior to rescue her fallen friend, completely drained, and she wet herself. The thing moved a little, and she saw that it was feeding on a small mammal that must have been stupid enough to get too close to it.

The lesson was not lost on her.

She slid the pistol from her waistband and slowly began to step backwards, careful to shift her weight very gradually, lest she inadvertently snap a twig or kick a stone, bringing the thing's alien-like jaws snapping straight at her.

She felt bracken sink into the soft earth under her weight and could feel her heart hammering in her chest. She had been an idiot to come back here looking for Winters. She wasn't a trained warrior. She wasn't a hero. She was just a dumb farmer who had made a stupid mistake.

Then, the centipede reared up, its head swinging this way and that, obviously alerted to some strange smell or sound.

Lai Anh swallowed a scream and jumped behind a nearby tree, pressing her back hard against the bark, pistol gripped tight in both hands. The Vietnam Black made a strange, sucking, chittering sound, as though it was sucking in air past a lump of phlegm, and she shut her eyes tight. Her heart beat faster, a clicking in her chest. She heard the undergrowth crumple under the beast's weight as the spike-like legs moved.

She nudged the safety off the M1911.

She didn't believe that the weapon would have the slightest effect against the Vietnam Black's armour plating, but perhaps she could stick a round in its eye, or jam the barrel into its mouth. Even if the thing did survive, even if the rounds still failed to penetrate its chitinous body, she imagined how satisfying pulling the trigger would be. The hardest punch in the face that she could deliver.

And if that didn't work, then she could always save one bullet for herself.

She opened her eyes.

The monster was right by the tree. She could see the twitching of its antennae just in the corner of her vision. If it turned its head, it would see her. Again, that phlegmy hiss came.

She changed grip on the pistol and prepared to make her move.

Suddenly, with a contralto rumbling sound, the Vietnam Black spun around and thrust itself in the opposite direction. A high-pitched, startled cry sounded in the stillness, and Lai Anh screwed her eyes shut again. Another small mammal - a rabbit, a monkey, perhaps - had been unlucky enough to stumble into the centipede while it was searching for her. She slowly leaned around the tree and could see the ropey, muscular form of the creature wrapped around its new prize. A small black paw reached up feebly, fingers clutching and clasping for any assistance, its muscles and cartilage spasming in pain as the foul toxin of the monster seeped in.

The whistling breath of the Vietnam Black fell quieter again, as did the mewling of the monkey it had caught. Lai Anh relaxed a little, confident that the creature was once again satisfied with its meal. She stepped back from the tree she had been hiding behind and her gaze fell upon what the thing had been eating when she had first arrived. She slapped her hand to her mouth to stop herself from screaming.

Sergeant Reese lay dead, his stomach cut away, torn and spread by the mandibles of the Vietnam Black. She saw now the wake of the broken branches and bracken where the thing had dragged him through the undergrowth. His eyes were staring up blankly, as if trying to get a final glimpse of the sunlight through the thick canopy above them.

She wretched, and a dribble of vomit spurted between her fingers, which caused her to gag again, the pulped up, acid-tinged remnants of the US forces rations spilling over her hands and onto the jungle floor. She saw the Vietnam Black move a little in the background and did her best to suppress the urge to cough or groan. It didn't seem to have noticed her yet, but she didn't want to make herself a target either.

She shuffled backwards another step, then another. The monster let out a breathy hiss that was almost a sigh, and seemed to stop moving.

The monkey's fingers twitched twice more, then froze still.

Two more steps, and she felt safe enough to risk a little noise. She thumbed the safety back into position on the pistol, turned, and ran full pelt in the direction she had come. She knew that there was every chance she could hit a land mine, pull over tripwire, or catch the attention of a passing tiger, but all of those felt preferable to falling under the legs and fangs of the Vietnam Black.

She ran blindly, powered only by adrenaline, panic, and the haunting memory of Sergeant Reese's final resting place.

Would the monster return for seconds once it had consumed the monkey?

Did it matter if it did?

Her run came to an abrupt halt as she collided with the muscled chest of Walton. She bounced off of him cartoonishly and fell onto her backside. Relief flooded through her, and she started crying, her body not sure how to process the rollercoaster of emotions she had been on. She felt Walton and Hanson lift her up to her feet.

"Lai Anh?" asked Hanson. "Where did you go? Where have you been?"

"I…I went back," she said.

Hanson's confusion was only temporary. His face softened. "For Winters?"

"Yes. I did not find him."

"Did you see anything else?"

She swallowed and wiped the tears from her eyes. "No. I saw no-one. Nothing. There is nothing behind us. We should go on."

"Did you see it?"

She swallowed again. "No."

"Something scared you, Lai Anh. What was it?"

"Nothing. I got lost. It reminded me of when I was a small girl and I got lost in the jungle. I got frightened. I ran. I found you. That is all."

Hanson and Walton exchanged a look, then Hanson nodded. "Okay. Maybe you should walk in the middle of us from now on. That way we can keep an eye out for you in every direction."

"I would like that."

***

They marched on until their stomachs began to growl as the sun set. They set up a camp, cooked up a shitty meal from left over rations, and it was very little time at all before Lai Anh was curled up on the ground asleep.

"Do you know where we're heading next?" Hanson asked, so quietly he was barely audible over the chirps of the insects, the haunting screeches and growls of the jungle.

Walton nodded. "Another two hours in the direction we're going and we should hit a small river. From there, we can just follow it straight back to the base. It's the one that passes right around the back of the canteen. You know where I mean?"

"Yeah, I know it. It's that easy huh?"

Walton lit a cigarette. "Nah, man. It'll be just as hard a slog as the jungle, but - hoping to god here - it won't be as hot. We'll at least get a nice breeze coming off of the water that'll stop it feeling so much like a fucking sauna as it does in here. Don't get me wrong, the walk is still going to be long and hard...unless..."

"Unless what?"

"Unless we manage to grab ourselves a ride. Maybe we can pay off a fisherman or something, and take a nice cruise back to base. Frankly, I've had a shitty few days, and a little river ride would do my spirits a lot of good."

Hanson considered it. "I guess we could try. Ain't got much to bribe him with, though."

"I got a few bucks and a pack of smokes. Plus he'll have the chance to ogle Lai Anh for a couple of hours. I think I can cut a bargain with some desperate gook; or, at least, his teenage son."

"Okay. We'll try, but if it don't work, we're back to travelling on foot."

"Yup."

Hanson sat back, supporting his weight behind him on his palms. Walton had to suppress a giggle at the thought that he looked like he was relaxing in the park or at the beach back home, and the mental image of the corporal in his trunks and holding a bottle of lemonade popped into his mind for no reason. Man, he was even more tired that he thought he was.

After a second, Corporal Hanson asked "How hot is this river?"

"No hotter than the jungle."

"Come on, man, you know what I mean."

"Yeah, I do; and like I say, it's no hotter than the jungle. It's probably crawling with Charlie and Nathaniel Victor, but at the same time, it's going to be harder for them to engage us there."

"How so?"

"Charlie likes to lay traps. Charlie likes to dig in and wait for you so he can ambush you once you're within six inches of his hole. With Charlie, the jungle is his weapon. You don't see him until he's on you."

"Sounds like someone else we've run into a couple of times."

"Right. I don't think that big bug will like the water neither. Out in the sun? Most bugs can't stand bright light, that's why in your back yard they're always hiding under rocks and shit. Once we hit the river, I reckon he'll lose interest. Besides…how the fuck is he gonna swim?"

CHAPTER SIXTEEN

Walton was as good as his word, and it was almost exactly two hours after breakfast (another shitty K-Ration, of course) that they noticed the trees beginning to thin. From then, it was only another twenty minutes before they stepped out onto the muddy banks of a small river; probably no more than a hundred yards across, from bank to bank.

"No fishermen," muttered Hanson, throwing his cigarette butt down onto the mud. He only had one pack left, and was already frustrated knowing that he was going to have to pace himself. Darkly, he wondered if he should have taken Reese's smokes, along with the grenade launcher. "No boats."

Walton shrugged, the M60 pointing skyward. "So? We walk. Same as we have been doing all this time."

"Great."

"Look, we'll run into a boat sooner or later. These gooks are half fish, you know that? Most of them can't stand to be away from the river for more than a couple of hours. Makes them dry out and go all scaly. Like this one here." He laughed, and slapped Lai Anh on the arm.

"I can't swim," she replied.

Walton shut up, and the three of them began the trudge down the bank of the river, the mud sucking at their boots every step of the way. Lai Anh gave up with her sandals after only a hundred feet or so, and flung them into the river in frustration, continuing the rest of the way barefoot.

"No snakes here, huh?" joked Walton.

"Yes. Many...but sandals don't stop snakes."

She had a point.

***

It was half an hour later that they spotted the boat.

A ramshackle jetty poked out of the mud, with a dilapidated wooden hut set several yards further back - far enough that it wouldn't be affected by a rising tide or reasonable sized flood. The boat itself looked similarly beaten up. A hammered together central cabin looked like it wouldn't be able to resist a strong wind, but it would at least provide protection from the heat of the Vietnam sun.

"Reckon he'll be up for giving us a ride?" asked Walton, sweat running down his forehead.

"We can ask, I guess. No harm in trying."

They crossed the muddy bank to the shack, and as they approached, they saw the lone occupant stand up and watch them. Hanson raised his hands to show that his rifle was slung, although Walton's large weapons prevented him from doing so. Still, the man held up his own arms in reply.

"English?" shouted Hanson. The man was backlit by the morning sun, and he couldn't make out his features.

"A little," shouted back the voice, high and reedy.

Lai Anh shouted out to him in Vietnamese, and the voice replied to her, much more confident this time, and at greater length. She smiled at Hanson and Walton. "You forget I was here?"

"Does he sound friendly?"

"I guess so. He isn't aggressive."

They slowly approached the hut, and Hanson wiped sweat from his forehead. "Ask him if he can sail down the river for us."

They were much nearer now, and the man had walked out of the shadow of his shack. He was pretty old, Hanson saw, easily in his late sixties or early seventies, a life of hardship etching lines across his face. The beginnings of a hunched back were just beginning to show, as the weight of the years had piled upon his shoulders. He had a kindly face, though, and smiled widely at them.

Lai Anh spoke several words in Vietnamese and the man looked apologetic, throwing his hands up and replying slowly.

"He says his wife is ill, and he cannot leave her," Lai Anh translated. "He is very sorry, but he cannot help."

"Fuck," muttered Walton. "Ask him if there are any other boats around here. I don't wanna fucking walk if I don't have to."

Another flurried exchange, and Lai Anh shook her head. "He said there is a neighbour down the shore another five hundred yards or so, but he doesn't think it is in very good repair. His neighbour is a lazy man who doesn't care for his boat."

The man yammered away again.

Lai Anh chuckled. "He says that his neighbour claims a sea monster smashed the underside of his boat, and since then he has been too scared to go back out in it."

The two men did not laugh. If the Vietnam Black was real, then they saw no reason to laugh at the notion of sea monsters ripping the hull from a boat. They could laugh when they were back, safe and sound, asleep in their bunks.

Hanson lit a cigarette. He was running low, but he'd deal with that when it became a real problem. "Can we hire his boat? Maybe he can use the money for some medicine for his wife? We have money and we have smokes. Put the emphasis on the money, though."

Lai Anh and the old man spoke. Walton leaned over to Hanson and said, "Reckon there is a wife, or do you think he just doesn't want to be seen with American troops? Charlie could be keeping an eye on him."

Hanson shrugged. "If he rents us the boat, he can lie about whatever he wants."

"Bradley would have said to smoke him and we take the boat."

"Bradley's dead."

Walton nodded. "Shame about Grandpa."

"The New Guy?"

"Yeah. He was okay, and that ain't no way for anyone to die."

"Yeah. What was his name again?"

"I can't remember. We just called him Grandpa."

Lai Anh had finished with the fisherman. "He is willing to lend us his boat, for the right price. He wants to know what we're offering."

Hanson looked to Walton.

"Strapped, huh?" asked the large man.

"Quit stalling. What have you got?"

He fumbled through his pockets. "Twenty bucks and two packs of smokes."

"Offer him ten and one pack, Lai Anh."

Another incomprehensible exchange passed between them before Lai Anh translated. "Fifteen. He's not interested in the cigarettes."

"You got change for fifteen there, Walton?"

"Fuck no, man. Two tens."

Hanson smirked, and turned to Lai Anh. "Twenty, and he shows us how the damn thing works."

***

It was about half an hour later that they were finally ready to launch into the river. The man had been very thorough, and they had picked up the controls easily enough.

The engine took two or three tries before it eventually turned over, but when it finally did, it came to life with a powerful roar that made them feel confident and powerful.

Hanson, who had some boating experience - nothing major, but he'd been out on his Grandad's boat a few times - had the wheel. Anticipating trouble, Walton stood up by the prow of the ship, his M60 resting on the edge as a makeshift turret. It was a sensible decision, reflected Hanson. They were still deep in NVA and Viet Cong territory, and it would be stupidity to drop their guard now.

Lai Anh sat on the floor, half asleep.

Hanson played a game with himself, pretending that they were just out on a pleasant cruise; a bunch of friends enjoying the summer vacation. He was at the wheel of a fishing boat they'd rented, and they'd driven off the coast of Florida for some rest and relaxation. That wasn't a machine gun Walton was carrying; it was a fishing pole, and he was going to catch them some sea bass for their dinner tonight. Lai Anh had had too many beers and was dozing on the floor beside them. She'd wake up soon and they'd all joke and laugh with her for being so silly as to fall asleep and miss out on the fishing.

He wished they had some music. The Stones or Creedence Clearwater would go down really well, right about now. He also wished they had some beers, that would make the illusion complete.

He wasn't normally one to day dream, but the events of the past few days had been such a nightmare that it was nice, even if only to dream for a little while.

He checked his pocket. Three cigarettes left. Better pace himself. He could always beg some from Walton, but he'd end up paying for that in the long run.

Lai Anh yawned noisily.

"Why don't you get some sleep?" he asked. "We've got at least a couple of days before we get back to the base. I'll wake you when we get there."

The girl nodded, and closed her eyes. "What will happen to me when I get to where we're going?" she asked, dreamily.

Hanson had been so concerned with getting them to the river, he hadn't stopped to think about that. It seemed almost selfish to him, in a way. He'd had a bad mission, but this girl had had her whole life destroyed over the past few days. She had no home to go back to.

"I don't know, but they'll look after you. They'll probably want to talk to you about Dr. Xuan, and any Viet Cong you saw in the area. They'll probably want to know more about the Vietnam Black, too. After that, I guess they'll turn you over to the Red Cross, or something like that."

"What is the Red Cross?"

"They're sort of doctors. They'll check you over and makes sure you're healthy, then they'll...find somewhere for you to go."

"Can I choose where they'll send me?"

"I don't think they can make you go somewhere that you really don't want to go, but I don't know that you can just go wherever you want."

"Okay."

A moment of silence passed before he called out to Walton. "Any sign of anything out there, Walton?"

The big man kept sweeping his gaze from one side of the river to the other. "Nothing so far, but the trees come real close to the shoreline. There could be a whole battalion of gooks just twenty yards back and we wouldn't know a goddamn thing about it."

"Just keep them peeled and do the best you can, Walton."

"Always do."

He looked down. Lai Anh wasn't yet asleep, but her eyes had drooped half-closed. "Say, Walton, I just thought of something."

"What's that?"

"When we're finished, how are we going to get the fisherman's boat back to him?"

Walton laughed. "Oh, please. We bought this."

"What do you mean?"

"The man was practically a fucking antique. Those twenty bucks will mean he won't have to go fishing for a long damn time, and if he does outlive his riches, then...well...I'm sure he's got family he can call on for favours. He ain't expecting to see it back again."

"Huh. So I guess we own a boat, now."

"We'll be the envy of the base, man."

Lai Anh's voice rose up from the floor. "What is that?"

"What's what?" asked Hanson, instantly assuming for a moment that she'd seen Charlie, or the Centipede.

"There. That machine under the wheel."

Hanson ducked down and looked at what she was pointing at. "It's a radio! My god! Walton, there's a radio on board!"

"Cool. Put some tunes on."

"Not that kind of radio! A two way! We can call for an evac!"

"Do it, man! What are you waiting for!"

Hanson gestured for Lai Anh to take the wheel, which she did, nervously. He tinkered with the handset and the dials for a while before punching into what he thought was the frequency used by their home base. "Base Romeo Golf Papa, Base Romeo Golf Papa, this is Corporal Mike Hanson, from Sergeant Reese's squad. We have taken heavy casualties, and have a…rescued hostage. We require evac ASAP."

A minute passed, and he repeated the message.

This time, a response came through, thin and distorted. "Receiving you, Corporal Hanson. What are the extent of your injuries?"

"Romeo Golf Papa, we have one civilian in shock and four dead personnel, including the commanding officer. We are currently sailing down a river in a commandeered craft, but we're not certain how seaworthy it is. We are low on supplies, and low on ammo. We need evac."

"Corporal Hanson, how long can you hold out?"

"We have one belt of M60 ammo, two clips of M16 ammunition, three rounds for an M79, plus sidearms. Little food and even less in terms of medical supplies. Charlie could be anywhere. We're comfy, but we won't be for long."

He gave them their estimated location, though he knew a lot of it would come down to guesswork and hunting them down on the part of the chopper pilot. That couldn't be helped. They needed to keep moving, and as the only boat in sight on the river, they should stick out like a sore thumb to the Huey.

The problem was that they also stuck out to Charlie and his friends.

The radio fell silent for a moment, before the operator came back. "Corporal Hanson, keep moving downriver. We'll have a Huey out to you in approximately three hours."

"Romeo Golf Papa, thank you. We'll keep an eye out for you and pop smoke when we see you."

"Stay safe, Corporal. We'll see you soon. Over and out."

Walton looked over his shoulder. "What did they say?"

"They said a chopper's on its way. We should be home for dinner."

"Damn. I was hoping the canteen would be closed by the time we got there."

"A man can dream, Walton."

He took the wheel back from Lai Anh, who wasted no time to trying to get to sleep again. He decided that was a good idea, and slipped back into his comfortable, warm dream of a fishing trip, out on the ocean waves with his friends.

Walton interrupted him. "Hey, man. How about we switch places. I'm getting bored as shit up here. I wanna have a go of driving the boat."

"You don't drive a boat, you sail it. That you don't know that is why I'm not gonna let you."

"Aw, man. You're no fun."

"Shut up and catch me something good for dinner."

"Man, there ain't nothing in this river but crocs and gook shit."

***

It watched them from the tree line, the distinctive purring chug of the Diesel engine easy to follow. It reached the water and slipped in, its forty-two legs swimming easily through the murky muddy water. Its whole body was muscle and cartilage, pure whipcord strength.

Its antenna twitched and picked up on the ripples and vibrations of the small fishing boat.

CHAPTER SEVENTEEN

They had been sailing quietly and uninterrupted for just over an hour when the boat suddenly jolted hard to the side. Hanson was thrown off balance, stumbled, and would have fallen were it not for having kept a tight hand on the wheel. He reflexively spun it back in the direction of the jolt, exactly as he would have done to get out of a skid in a car, and the boat rocked hard back on course. For a moment he felt like a pirate in a children's book, sailing the rough seas of the old world.

Lai Anh had been fast asleep when the impact came and she went rolling across the cabin behind him. Her head collided with the wall and she grunted in pain and annoyance. "What was that?" she asked, still half-asleep.

"I dunno. Maybe the bottom scraped a rock or something."

Walton came running in. "What the fuck was that? Did we hit a mine or something?"

"We don't float mines in the river, man. We probably just hit a rock or something. Where's your gun?"

"Out front, on the deck, man. Whatever it was we hit, we hit it pretty hard."

Lai Anh stood, shakily. "Are we sinking?"

Walton and Hanson exchanged glances. Walton shook his head. "We're back level again. We kept moving. I mean, I'm no sailor, but how bad can it be?"

"Go look below," said Hanson, turning his attention back to the wheel. He dropped the speed. He didn't think there was any point rushing ahead if they were in mortal danger...or would they be better off charging ahead full steam for as long as they could before beaching the boat? He didn't know. He'd never been in charge before.

"I'll go," said Lai Anh, dropping through a trap door in the cabin.

"I didn't even know that was there," muttered Walton.

"Go back up front. We're moving a lot slower, now, so we're sitting ducks if Charlie spots us."

Walton grunted an acknowledgement, lit a cigarette and left the cabin.

Lai Anh clambered back up into the cabin after a few minutes. "No water. No damage. I think we're okay."

Hanson nodded, studying the tree line on either side of them. "Good. You know for a moment, I was just thinking that everything was going okay, and then that happened. I guess it goes to show that you should never take things for gran-"

The boat rocked again, this time in the other direction.

Hanson spun the wheel to correct the balance of the boat once again.

Walton turned over his shoulder and shouted to him. "We gotta beach, man! Something dangerous is underneath us, and we're gonna get fucked up if we stay here!"

Hanson looked up to shout his agreement, when he completely froze.

Lai Anh made a whimpering sound.

Walton saw the expressions on their faces, and knew what he was going to see as soon as he turned. He did so slowly, feeling as though his head was made of stone.

Rearing up in front of the boat, easily another four feet above his head, dripping with muddy river water, its thorny legs gripping the sides of the boat, was the Vietnam Black. It regarded him with piggy, black eyes, its antenna slowly waving back and forth, feeling him out with some sixth sense beyond human comprehension.

He saw the alienesque mouth part flex slowly, a strange black saliva-like substance oozing from them. Above those and more terrifying still: the mandibles. He had already seen what those crushing, piercing, scythes could do.

He couldn't move.

The thing made a strange, sighing, yawning noise as it swayed hypnotically above him. Suddenly, it reared back to strike, like a cobra.

In that split second of its motion, some primal survival instinct managed to penetrate his fear, and Walton could move again. He snatched up his M60, braced it, and squeezed the trigger. He yelled a wordless battle cry as the mechanical chucka-chucka-chucka of the belt-fed machine belched forth. He revelled in the percussive sound it made and the bright muzzle flash, but most of all cheered as the thing was knocked backwards and off balance.

Its sigh became a screech and he saw two, three legs sheared off by the 7.62mm bullets leaving the barrel at six hundred rounds a minute. It thrashed and squealed under his assault. Knocked off balance by the attack, its legs released, and it crashed back under the water.

Hanson and Lai Anh hurried to his side, brandishing their own weapons, but it was long gone.

"It is dead?" Lai Anh asked, shakily.

"Did you kill it?" asked Hanson.

Walton dropped the machine gun and slumped down onto the deck, his adrenaline fading fast. "I don't know. I...I don't think so. It didn't bleed much. I think I just knocked it off balance. Made it think twice, though."

"Yeah. It didn't like that you put up a fight. Guess it's used to being the top of the food chain."

Lai Anh was looking around nervously. "It will be back."

Walton picked up on the tone of her voice and got back to his feet. "No doubt. We need something with a bit more firepower."

"We can't risk the grenade launcher at this range," said Hanson. "If it comes up as close as that again, the grenades will take out the goddamn boat, not to mention the three of us with it."

"Man, it's getting to the point where I don't care. I just want that thing dead."

"I care. I care about getting Lai Anh over to the Red Cross. I care about getting your dumb ass home. I care about getting back to a proper bed, and I care about going home to my wife. If I gotta die in service of my country, then I gotta die in service of my country, but I'm not gonna die because you wanted to squish a bug."

Walton stopped, chuckled, and turned to smile at him. "It's a hell of a bug, though, ain't it?"

"The M-16s do nothing, the rounds just bounce off. The M60 seems to hurt it at weak points, but it's a goddamn tank, Walton. The grenades are too dangerous to use right here, right now."

"You wanna call in a goddamn air strike?"

"Cut the shit. We need melee weapons. If we can get a machete or an axe or something, I think we could stick it in between its armour plates. Those things are tough, but inside, it's just pulp, meat and gristle, right? Hell, maybe we could stick a spear straight down its throat."

"And where are we going to find shit like that on a boat in the middle of the goddamn river, Hanson?"

"There's gotta be something like that. It's a fishing boat. You stay up here, and keep watch. Lai Anh and I will go have a look and see what we can find."

***

Hanson searched below deck, while Lai Anh explored the sides of the boat, around the ramshackle cabin. She had seen netting, weights and other pieces of fishing equipment there, so assumed that there had to be more.

The netting was cold, wet and stank of river water. She knew that she'd be smelling it on her fingers for days to come. The rough, slimy rope oozed foul water over her hands with each movement. She suppressed a shudder and slowly pulled it aside, hoping to spot something useful.

There, lodged between the net and a crate of what smelt like rancid fish guts, was a large bladed knife, like some sort of machete. She supposed it must have originally been used for opening up especially recalcitrant crustaceans. There were spots of rust and muddy water stains running up the blade, but there was a weight to it that was satisfying. She raised it up above her head and swung it down into the rail that topped the waist-high wall that ran the perimeter of the deck.

It sunk about an inch into the swollen, damp wood, with a satisfying thud.

Still sharp.

She took it with her and looked around to see what else she could find.

Further down towards the rear of the boat, propped up against the exterior of the cabin, she found a six foot long pole topped with a wicked looking barbed spike. She had no idea what the original owner of the boat must have used it for, and to her eyes it looked decidedly military. She had no boating experience though, and supposed that it must have some perfectly innocent use - hooking the net when it was full at the end of the day, maybe? She grabbed the makeshift weapon by the haft, and turned to return to Walton at the front of the boat.

There, slithering up over the rail and onto the deck, was the front half of the Vietnam Black. It had only been six feet behind her while she considered the spear, and she hadn't heard a sound.

More segments moved sinuously up onto the deck, some missing legs, some scored from previous battles, and all glistening an oily black. Its head twitched from side to side, and she knew that it was painfully close to finding her. The strange radar sense it seemed to possess had her marked for death.

She dropped the machete with a clatter, and gripped the spear in both hands.

As soon as the blade bounced on the floor, the centipede's head flashed in her direction, its mandibles opening with a devilish hiss. Her blood ran cold, and she screamed.

The thing lashed toward her and she thrust forward with the spear, hoping that it was a heroic lunge that would take the spear point straight down the monstrous thing's throat, leaving it twitching and dying at her feet.

Instead, the Vietnam Black darted sideways, and wound its head to double back, catching the haft of the spear in the scything mandibles. The wood splintered with a damp crack and the spear point fell uselessly to the deck. Lai Anh tried jabbing feebly with the splintered point, but it just bounced harmlessly off of the thing's devilish head. It swiped sideways with a head butt, and the pole was knocked from her hands, over the deck rail and into the river.

The monster regarded her with a cold, dead glare.

Lai Anh closed her eyes and waited for the end to come.

The distinctive bark of Walton's M60 ripped through the air towards her. She looked up at the Vietnam Black. It squealed and turned quickly in Walton's direction. The Vietnam Black now blocked the whole gangway and it was impossible to see him, but she could still hear the machine gun barking and barking. The Vietnam Black hissed and thrashed as the bullets thudded into it.

With a scratching squeal that she had not heard before, it turned and went as if to climb back into the river, but instead stopped just short of the waterline. It ran along the side of the boat parallel to the river, keeping out of Walton's line of fire. Walton shouted, desperately trying to get a bead on it, but it was just out of his field of vision. Lai Anh grabbed the machete from where it had fallen and dashed to the rail, flailing wildly in an attempt to at least catch one of its legs with the blade, but it was moving too fast, and just out of her reach.

When the thing reached Walton it ran back over the rail again and shot forward, jabbing hard and fast, mandibles wide open. Walton skipped back quickly, shouting now for Hanson to come up and help. The M60 fired twice, three times, and she saw a round successfully clip it between the armour plates. It let out a hideous howl and goopy, black blood poured out.

The thing thrust forward again, and she saw fear in Walton's eyes. His ammo belt was running low.

She screamed and ran toward the centipede, raising the machete high above her head.

In a second, Hanson was there, catching her with one arm, and throwing her behind him. She fell hard to the deck, the machete skittering away from her.

Hanson brought his M16 to his shoulder and shouted for Walton to get out of the way, but it was all too late. The Vietnam Black's savage mandibles struck hard, catching Private Walton just at the bottom of his rib cage. The big man let out a savage roar of primal rage and pain as his olive green shirt became instantly stained with dark red blood. Hanson and Lai Anh joined him in the cry before being drowned out by the bark of Hanson's rifle.

As before, the rounds seemed to just glance from the monster's glistening black armour, but one bullet - far more by luck than judgement - caught the thing full in an eye. The Vietnam Black made a strangled groaning sound - unlike any of the hisses and clicks they had heard it make before, and dropped Walton to the deck. Black blood running from its destroyed eye socket, the monster turned and dove back into the muddy water of the river.

Lai Anh and Hanson instantly ran over to their fallen comrade, fearing the worst.

Walton was still conscious, and had wrapped his forearms to the wounds on either side of his rib cage as best as he could. "I need pressure and I need it now!" he shouted. "Hanson, push down on my right side. Lai Anh. See if there's any first aid supplies in the cabin."

"You don't really think there's going to be bandages in this rotten old shit hole, do you?" said Hanson, pressing down on the wound as hard as he could. "Did it catch you on the ribs or below them?"

"I dunno, man. A bit of both, I guess. I think the bottom one on this side is busted. Hey, that was a nice shot, by the way. Reckon that'll put him off for good this time?"

"Nah, man. I don't think we're that lucky. He knows you're wounded. He's coming back."

"I don't intend to be an easy dinner for the son of a bitch."

Lai Anh came back onto the deck, and shook her head. She hadn't found anything, just as Hanson had expected. He gestured for her to take his position. She hesitated for a nanosecond, then nodded, and slapped her hands over the gunner's wound. Blood leaked a little past her palms. She weighed a lot less than Hanson did.

Hanson jumped up, yanked off his t-shirt and with the aid of his combat knife cut his shirt into strips. He quickly improvised a bandage, which he and Lai Anh tied around Walton's chest.

"How do you feel?" he asked.

"Like shit."

"It doesn't look like that thing managed to poison you. The others reacted really quickly once they were bitten."

"I don't think the big things...mandibles, scythes, biters, whatever...I don't think they're poisoned. It's almost like they're a weapon, but the poison is delivered by its teeth, or maybe the legs, even. Or I'm lucky. Or...well, worst case scenario...it's just slow to act on me."

"We'll get you checked out back at base, soon. We'll be home before we know it. Another two hours, and the Huey'll be here."

CHAPTER EIGHTEEN

It was only another twenty minutes before they started taking fire.

At first they heard the popping of bullets and weren't sure where they were coming from or who they were being aimed at. Distant machine gun fire always sounded to Hanson like popcorn, and it usually took him a second to realise what it was. Gunfire never sounded like it did in the movies, all lively rattles and explosions. Real life gunfire was flat and dead.

Lai Anh instantly looked up and to the shore line, trying to see if there was anything to see. Walton, laying slumped against the side of the boat, the only comfortable position he could find with his two massive stab wounds, hissed at her to get down.

"But where are they?" she asked.

"Who knows? But if they can see us, the last thing you want to do is to give them a target, right?"

She shrugged, the cockiness of youth emboldening her. She craned her neck back up over the side of the boat, squinting across the river. "I don't see any-"

The bullets thudded into the side of the boat in a cluster of five percussive thuds. Wood splinters and dust were instantly thrown up into the air, and Lai Anh yelped, diving back into cover and throwing her hands over her head.

Walton laughed, then hissed in pain as it caused him to tug at the still barely congealed wounds on his sides. "Can't say I didn't warn you!"

Hanson came running into the cabin, and dropped to one knee in a skid. "Charlie. It's gotta be goddamn Charlie."

"That or our own boys taking a shot at us."

Hanson crawled on his belly over to Lai Anh and checked that she was okay. She'd a couple of grazes from falling hard onto the rough wood of the deck, but that was all. He made sure his helmet was fastened on tight, and then crept up to the side of the boat. Slowly, he raised his head, keeping his movement as steady and slight as possible. When he could just see over the side rail, he counted two seconds, then dropped back out of sight again.

"I can't see shit, man. There's nothing but fucking trees on that side."

"Charlie loves his jungle," muttered Walton, lighting a cigarette.

"We're never going to be able to return fire. We don't have the ammo for suppressive fire, and we can't pick out targets."

Another flurry of rounds struck the side of the boat heralding another yelp from Lai Anh. There were more of them this time, a semi-automatic burst.

"Lai Anh! Stay down!" Hanson yelled.

The firing stopped, and the silence afterwards was deafening.

"What the hell made them fire on us?" Hanson shouted across to Walton. "We just look like a goddamn fishing boat. They can't possibly have seen us from that distance!"

Walton was looking paler than normal. Hanson knew that he was suffering the effects of his wounds much more than he was letting on. "The radio."

"What do you mean?"

"When we radioed ahead for the evac, they must have intercepted the signal. They knew we were coming down the river at around this time. They're just attacking because we're a weak target."

"We need to get out of here."

"We're not gonna get much more speed out of this piece of shit engine."

Another round thudded into the deck. "They can keep this up forever. They could crawl on their hands and knees and keep pace with us."

Lai Anh crawled over to him. "Could we steer closer?"

"Why would we want to do that?"

Lai Anh nodded to the grenade launcher. "If we get closer, can't you use that?"

"Sure, but I still don't think we could see them. The trees are too goddamn thick."

Walton shouted as another hail of bullets peppered the hull. "It might make them think twice, at least."

Hanson nodded to him, then turned to whisper to Lai Anh. "Walton can't stand. He's gonna want to, because he's gonna want to play the hero. We can't let him. It'll tear up his insides worse than they already are. You understand me?"

Lai Anh nodded.

"Good. Okay, here's what we're going to do. I'm going to count three, and then you're going to run for the wheel, okay?"

They both ducked as a handful of rounds hit the deck, sending splinters of damp wood into the air.

"Okay."

"While you're doing that, I'm going to empty a clip in their direction. That'll make them put their heads down while you grab the wheel and steer the ship in their direction. As soon as you've given the wheel a little nudge, you drop to the floor and crawl back to me or to Walton, okay?"

"Okay."

"You're a brave girl, Lai Anh."

"I'm a girl with nothing to lose."

Hanson smirked. "Okay. Ready?"

"Yes."

"One. Two. Three!"

Lai Anh got to her feet and dashed for the wheel. Hanson sat up and fired off several rounds into the treeline. He couldn't pick out individual targets, but he could see little dashes and flickers of motion as the Viet Cong insurgents ran and ducked amongst the vegetation.

The rifle juddered and thudded against his shoulder as he fired off some wild shots, only trying to stop the Viet Cong from returning fire, not expecting to actually hit any of the targets.

It was only a split second before the Viet Cong returned fire and he was forced to duck back down behind the side of the boat. He rolled to the side to see how Lai Anh had fared.

She had fallen just short of the cabin door, and lay on her side, blood seeping from a gunshot wound in her leg.

Hanson felt ice cold adrenaline flood his nervous system. He crawled over to her and grabbed her hand. "Lai Anh? Can you hear me?"

She groaned, and looked at him, nodding. He hurriedly pulled her hands away and examined the wound. It wasn't bad. It looked like just a glancing blow - the bullet hadn't actually penetrated. "You're okay. It's a near miss, and it looks bloody, but there's no real damage. You should be walking on it by tomorrow. Do you understand?"

"It hurts!"

"Yeah, it hurts. It fucking sucks, but you'll be okay."

The boat was still sailing steady.

"The fuck do we do, Walton?" Hanson asked.

Walton flicked his cigarette butt away, and smiled, dozily. The blood loss was making him act like he was stoned. "Well, I was thinking...the radio got us into this mess, maybe it could get us out of it."

Hanson bandaged up Lai Anh's bullet graze as best he could. He hadn't been lying when he said that she should heal up pretty fast. "The chopper's already on its way, Walton. Radioing ahead isn't going to make it move any faster."

"Yeah, but there's things that can fly faster than a Huey, man."

It dawned on Hanson what the man was talking about. "A fire order? I can try, but would they go that far out here? Besides, Charlie can just intercept the radio signal again."

"And if he does, what the fuck is he going to do about it, man? Charlie can't outrun a Phantom."

What did he have to lose?

Hanson checked on Lai Anh again, then crawled to the cabin, and grabbed the radio. "Romeo Golf Papa, this is Corporal Hanson. Do you copy?"

The radio crackled for what seem like an hour before a reply came. "Corporal Hanson, this is Romeo Golf Papa. The Iriquouis are inbound. Is there a change to your situation?"

"We are taking fire from a Viet Cong patrol. We can barely see them in the trees. Could really do with some covering fire."

"Stand by Corporal Hanson."

"Standing by."

Walton lit his final cigarette and shouted. "This whole fucking war is 'standing by'. You're either standing around waiting to be shot at, or standing around while some prick shoots at you."

The radio came back to life before Hanson could formulate a reply.

"This is Romeo Golf Papa. We have two Thunderchiefs performing a patrol in the area. Can you mark the location with smoke?"

"Uh…we can try."

Walton hissed to get his attention. "Tell them we're laying red smoke."

"What? We can't throw red smoke that far. We ain't got any fucking smoke at all."

"Trust me. Tell him we're popping red smoke."

Hanson hesitated, then pressed the talk button. "We're popping red smoke."

"Roger. Barbecue on red smoke. Over and out, Corporal Hanson."

Hanson hung up the handset. "You mind telling me what that was all about?"

Walton nodded. "You got any cigarettes left?"

Hanson had barely any left, but threw him one anyway.

Walton lit it from his zippo and said, "You know why we don't announce what colour smoke we're using until the fly boys call it?"

Hanson had never really thought about it. The standard practice was to throw a coloured smoke grenade - red, for example. The pilots would then radio something like "We have red smoke", and you'd say "Confirm red smoke", and then they'd do whatever it was that you'd called them in to do. He'd never really thought as to why they should do it in that particular order. "No, why?"

"Because, back in the early days, we'd say something like "popping red smoke, target is two hundred yards east". Then the jets would come screaming in over the horizon, and Charlie would have been listening in over the radio and know that the bombs were going to come in two hundred yards east of wherever the red smoke was. Charlie may be many things, but he ain't stupid. What he'd do is he'd get every gook in radio range to pop a canister of red smoke. The Phantoms come along, and all they can see is a sea of red smoke from where every gook in the zip code has gotten in on the action."

"They muddied the signal."

"Right."

"I still don't get it. So why did we tell the cavalry that we'd be throwing red smoke?"

Walton smiled and nodded to something behind him. "Take a look."

Hanson spun around. A gulf of red smoke was billowing up from the trees to the port side of the boat.

Walton laughed. "Charlie doesn't know that we don't got any smoke. He's trying to muddy a signal that we aren't making…because he *is* the signal."

"Walton, you're a fucking genius."

"Ah, you're just saying that because it's true."

The Viet Cong seemed to have stopped firing for the moment. Hanson supposed that they must have been conserving their ammo; probably waiting for one of them to pop up to check that the coast was clear before cracking their heads open with a single bullet.

Hanson looked up and over the wall for a split second, then ducked back into cover. "The river narrows just ahead. It's less than a hundred yards or so across when we get up there."

"That's not good news if the gooks are following us, or if they have reinforcements."

"You think that's possible?"

"Is there red smoke up ahead? If there is, then that means that one of the gooks intercepted us earlier on and is trying to play smart. He's actually playing dumb, of course, but he ain't gonna know that before it's too late."

Hanson risked another quick glance, ducking back down just as a round caught the hull, reminding him that he daren't risk that too often.

"Yeah, about two hundred yards ahead."

"We need a back up plan."

Hanson shook his head. "I'm shit out of ideas, Lai Anh's no use and you're wounded."

"Hueys are on the way, man. We only need to wait them out."

Hanson had just begun to nod in agreement when the boat lurched hard to the right. He and Lai Anh slid and skidded across the deck, landing in a pile next to Walton.

"What the hell was that? Do they have an RPG?" he shouted.

"We hit a rock!" shouted Lai Anh. "The river is shallow here."

"Are we taking in water?"

"I…I don't know. We're not moving."

Walton rolled his eyes. "Great. We're beached."

Hanson groaned in frustration, and grabbed the M79 from where it had fallen. He stood, fired a grenade over to the opposite treeline, then another and another in rapid succession. Their explosions barked across the river, and they were close enough to feel the shockwave and heat. "Okay, run for the trees."

He and Lai Anh grabbed Walton, each throwing one of his arms over their shoulders, and helped him to his feet. Lai Anh paled briefly, but didn't make a sound. Hanson had forgotten what the extra weight would do to the gash on her leg.

He didn't know if the grenades he had fired had actually caused any casualties - in fact he thought it pretty unlikely - but they had done the work he intended for them to do and made Charlie duck his head down for a few seconds. The three of them jumped over the side of the fishing boat into the muddy river. The brackish water came midway up Hanson's calves, and was past Lai Anh's knees.

The water dragged at their legs and made their clothes heavier, making the short jog to the shore torturous. Hanson could only imagine how much worse it was for his two wounded colleagues.

They only managed four dragging steps through the water before they heard the popping of rifle fire again. Slower this time - definitely a bolt action rifle, rather than an AK-47. Perhaps they were out of ammo, or Hanson had gotten lucky with a grenade shot. Either the boat was still providing enough cover, or the shots were going wide, because he neither felt nor heard any bullets strike the water around them.

He looked back over his shoulder. The river was a hundred yards wide here, and he could see the men of the Viet Cong moving at the treeline. If he could see them, then he was a large enough a target for them to hit.

"We need to get to the trees!" he yelled. "If we get to the trees, we can hide out until the air support gets here. If we get stuck on the beach we're dead."

Then he heard clicking and hissing.

CHAPTER NINETEEN

The monster that had stalked them for days rose up from the murky river, regarding them with its one remaining eye. Silt and brown water ran down its shining black body in rivulets, making it look like some hideous monster grown from the trenches of the First World War. Its mandibles, washed clean now of Walton's blood, opened wide, an alien rattling noise emerging from its twitching, oozing mouth.

It reared up to a height of ten feet, towering above them, and Hanson felt a strange Tinnitus like white noise build up in his ears, blocking out everything else around him, and he wondered if this meant that he was about to die.

The M60 was back in the boat.

There hadn't been time to grab it, and even if there had been, there was no way they could have carried it and Walton's weight too. He had his M16 on his back, but there was no way he could reach it with Walton in the way.

This was how they were going to die.

Lai Anh's roar of anger and aggression broke through the whistling in his ears, and it took him a moment to realise that she was shouting in Vietnamese, rather than just screaming. The harsh consonants conveyed her anger better than a scream of pure rage would have. She had pulled the automatic pistol he had given her earlier from the waistband of her pants and was squeezing rounds off at the centipede.

Although the bullets were not exactly large calibre, at this range they were enough that the centipede was rocked with each hit, flinching and ducking as they struck home.

The centipede lashed forward, mandibles snapping at them, forcing them to scatter. Lai Anh ran up onto the shore, towards the tree line. Hanson tried to support Walton, and danced back a few steps in the water. It was enough that the snake-like strike was off its mark, and the thing's head struck the river, harmlessly. Instantly it lashed back again, ready to strike, but by this time Walton had drawn his own sidearm one handed, and was trying to draw aim on it.

"Shoot the antennae!" hissed Hanson, struggling to help keep the big man upright.

"Never gonna make a shot like that..." Walton grumbled, but tried anyway. Hanson laughed as he saw a grey-black scratch mark appear across the top of the monster's head.

"You're getting pretty close!"

"Leave me here and run for the trees. Lai Anh has the right idea. I'm fucking slowing you down here, man!"

The Vietnam Black growled this time, swinging its sinuous body low; the sickle like mandibles now at waist height. Hanson had a momentary vision of what it would be like to be caught in their vice-like grip, crushing your hipbone, or cutting into your stomach.

Another bullet caught it in the side of the head, this time fired from the treeline. Lai Anh was just at the edge of the trees, firing in an attempt to distract the monster away from them.

The creature turned to look at her, obviously seeing her as more of a threat than the injured human in front of it, and dashed off after her, its myriad legs pushing it through the water and up the muddy bank with ease. Hanson was about to shout for her to run when a hail of bullets struck the trees where she was standing, and she fell to the ground, covering her head with her hands.

She had run to a spot past where the boat provided cover, and the Viet Cong had opened fire.

Walton and Hanson both screamed her name and began desperately splashing up the bank towards her, the tail end of the Vietnam Black swishing past them, causing more of the foul river water to splash up into their faces.

In a second, the Vietnam Black was towering over her. Hanson slipped over in the mud at the water's edge, and went face down, dragging Walton with him. He spat the silt from his mouth and clambered to his hands and knees, reaching back futilely for Walton.

"I'm okay! Get to Lai Anh!" The gunner screamed, propping himself up on one arm, and dragging himself upright.

Hanson nodded, grabbed his rifle from where it hung on his back and jogged up the incline towards her. He pulled the butt to his shoulder, sighted, and fired two three-round bursts - one into the trees above Lai Anh, and one into the monster itself. He saw Lai Anh try and roll further into the woods, and was relieved that she didn't seem to have been hit by the Viet Cong. The Vietnam Black turned and hissed at him, once more undulating and writhing across the ground towards him, its spike-looking legs sinking into the mud, but still propelling it ever forward.

He took aim at the things head once more when a large explosion burst from the mud just a few feet to the monster's side, near the river. He was knocked off of his feet and momentarily dazed. The ringing started up in his ears again and he had to shake his head violently to bring his surroundings back into focus. A large crater had been blown in the mud near the water's edge, and he could hear Vietnamese voices drifting across the river. The Viet Cong must have an RPG-7! A shoulder launched rocket propelled grenade! Their small arms fire had obviously failed to do the trick, so they had resorted to the big guns.

The centipede hissed out in anger, and Hanson noticed that now one antenna hung limply from a break halfway down. Two legs were also sheared off by the force of the explosion and one had sunk into the mud near his head, twitching spasmodically.

The Vietnam Black looked at him, then swung its gaze in the direction of the Viet Cong. Its legs danced back and forth a moment as it thought things through, and then it drove off, back into the river.

"It's going for Charlie!" screamed Walton, crawling up the mud bank. "Charlie pissed off the Việt Nam Đen!"

Hanson couldn't believe the speed the thing was making, barrelling through the water like a torpedo. A crack of rifle fire reminded him that he was still in range of the Viet Cong's guns, and he ducked his head low before running over to Lai Anh.

Walton made a beeline for the trees nearest to him, intending to circle round to them, giving him more cover from Charlie's attacks.

Lai Anh had been hit, but was still conscious. She had one hand clapped to her left side, and blood was seeping out between her fingers.

"Getting hit twice in one day is no fun," muttered Hanson, feeling compelled to try and joke with her. "Can you move?"

Lai Anh groaned in pain and gritted her teeth, but managed to nod weakly. "Is it bad?"

"It'd be bad if we had to move you or if we had to wait days for an evac, but don't forget that the chopper's going to be here any second. You don't have anything to worry about."

A bullet struck Hanson in the side of the head and he fell to the ground.

Lai Anh screamed and flopped onto her right side, her face slapping hard into the mud. Keeping one hand pressed to her wounded side, with the other she stretched out and clawed into the ground, pulling herself along in an awkward scrabbling crawl. The river mud slipped and slid under her fingers, and she was cold and filthy in seconds. She knew she had to get deeper into cover. Hanson was dead because he'd stopped to help her, and she had to get to safety, or his sacrifice meant nothing.

She heard Walton calling her name and looked up to see the gunner hobbling through the trees toward her. She called out his name in return and he spotted her in an instant. His lumbering jog became more agitated and he reached her in a few seconds. "Where's Hanson? Where is he?"

"Back there. He was hit."

"Is he dead?"

Lai Anh didn't want to say it. She just looked down at the ground, sadly.

"You're fucking kidding me. Hanson's gone?"

She screwed her eyes tight and nodded her head feebly.

"What happened?"

"I don't know. They shot him."

Walton took a deep breath. "Wait here."

Lai Anh's eyes popped back wide open. "Where are you going?"

"I'm going to check he's dead."

"He was hit by a bullet. Why don't you believe me?"

"I believe you that he's hit. We can't say for sure that he's dead. You wait here, let me go check."

Lai Anh reached out a hand to grab at him, to stop him from leaving her, but he was already gone.

***

Lai Anh had only managed to crawl ten feet or so, and Walton could see Hanson's body almost right away, laying in the treeline, in the sunlight. What the hell had he been thinking, stopping there, in plain view of the enemy?

He'd stopped to help Lai Anh, of course. Hanson would do anything for any of the squad, and Lai Anh had become a de facto member. Walton dropped down low, wincing at the pain from his wounded abdomen, and tried crawling slowly over to Hanson.

"Hanson? You okay?"

As he crawled along, his hand touched something hard in the otherwise soft mud. He looked down.

It was Hanson's helmet.

He picked it up and looked it over.

There was a large dent in one side of it, punched in more than an inch, the camouflage material ripped and a little scorched. He poked it with a fingertip. It hadn't been penetrated.

"Hanson! You hear me?"

The sound of gunfire again. He ducked his head but no bullets struck the area around them. More gunfire, but no impacts. He heard shouts and curses in Vietnamese drifting across the river. Glancing up, he could see ten or so Viet Cong at the treeline on the other side of the river, pointing and firing at something moving across the river towards them.

The Vietnam Black.

"Hanson, do you fucking hear me?"

Hanson raised a hand weakly and grunted something.

"You hurt?"

Walton felt his spirits lift as he saw the corporal raise his head slowly, his hair mussed and sweat soaked. Hanson looked left and right in confusion, eventually focusing on Walton. "The fuck happened?"

"Are you hurt?"

"Nothing feels broken. Where are we?"

"Lai Anh says you got shot. Looks to me like your helmet took the brunt of it. How do you feel?"

"Like I've been shot in the fucking head, Walton, how the fuck do you think I feel?"

"I think you're one of the only people to be shot in the head and live to tell the story, so how about you quit griping?"

"I like griping."

Walton chuckled. "Okay. Can you move?"

A thudding explosion came from the other side of the river, and they both glanced over just in time to see a gout of water shoot up from just past the halfway mark.

"The fuck are they doing?" asked Hanson, propping himself up on his elbows.

"They got bug trouble," said Walton. "Look, man, we gotta get hidden. They're not firing on us right now, but we're still in plain sight, here. We can't wait here forever."

He half threw, half rolled Hanson's helmet over to him. Hanson caught it and turned it over in his hands, examining the divot caused by the Viet Cong bullet. "I'm a hell of a lucky guy."

"You'll be a dead lucky guy if we don't get moving, come on!"

Screams of terror echoed across the water.

They both watched, dumbstruck, as the Vietnam Black rose out of the water, and lanced forward, wrapping its body around the nearest of the Viet Cong. The man's screams shot up a whole octave as the venom from its bite and legs rushed into his nervous system. The other men danced and scurried around him, squeezing fully automatic fire from AK-47s and hurriedly aimed shots from bolt action rifles.

The monster threw the dead man to the mud and whipped its tail around, knocking another to the floor, clutching his ribs. The rattling hiss echoed across the river, and it shot its wicked head forward again, biting down and completely bisecting one of the Viet Cong. His legs stayed upright for a moment, a fountain of red spraying upwards, before they fell forward onto their knees, then down into the mud.

"They're dead. They're all fucking dead if they don't run," whispered Hanson, shakily getting to his feet.

More Viet Cong poured out of the trees now. One lobbed a grenade, but he overshot his mark and it landed about ten feet behind the Vietnam Black, in the river. A fountain of brackish water shot upwards as the grenade detonated, but it didn't seem to even distract the centipede. Instead it whipped its head sideways, knocking one of the guerrilla fighters six feet up into the air, to be smashed and broken against a tree trunk.

One of the men, clearly marking himself out as the leader of the group, was gesturing wildly, ordering his men to try and circle the Vietnam Black. He was firing on it a pistol. They could see the muzzle flash clearly, but its retort was lost in the clamour of battle. A younger Vietnamese soldier charged bravely at the monster. Swinging what looked like a machete, he managed to hit it two, three times before the black mandibles closed around him, lifting him high into the air. He kicked and struggled for a few seconds, before falling lifeless in its grip.

The Vietnam Black cast him aside like a rag doll and let out a triumphant hiss. It turned its gaze on the leader, and the man visibly quaked. He snatched an AK-47 from a younger soldier next to him, shoving him violently aside.

"Just fucking run, man..." whispered Hanson. He had no love for the Viet Cong. It was hard to love a man who had just shot you in the head, but it wasn't a good feeling to see them cut down this way. It was something primal that went beyond the Vietnam War, beyond white and Asian, beyond democracy and communism. It was the horror of seeing the food chain reversed - witnessing insect feed on mammal.

Hanson turned away and staggered unsteadily over to Walton and helped the gunner to his feet, throwing his arm over his shoulder so that he could lean against him. It was the wounded leading the wounded, but a penetrating wound trumped a possible concussion every time.

"Do you think it'll come back for us once it's finished chewing on Charlie?" asked Walton, grunting as he took a step backwards.

"I don't think that we want to be here when it finishes. Choppers can't be too far away, right?"

CHAPTER TWENTY

The leader of the Viet Cong was only a young man himself, not yet thirty. He braced the butt of the AK-47 tight against his shoulder, and fired wildly. The thing breathed out a guttural snarl and thrust forward and back, snapping as it did so, testing his defences.

Hanson and Walton watched the man yell a challenge, just as the Vietnam Black balled up its muscles and then burst forward, enveloping the leader in a knot of carapace and legs. The man's screams carried the hundred yards across the water, and chilled them both to the bone. His men took his death as a direct affront, and redoubled their attack on the hideous invertebrate.

Then there came another screaming sound.

"You hear that?" asked Walton.

"I hear it. You know what that is?"

The screaming became an airy howl, and they felt their arm hairs start to rise.

Across the water, the centipede was unravelling, revealing a pulpy mass where the Viet Cong leader had once been. The thing was feeding now, burying its head in the young man's stomach, dripping blood and ichor to the muddy floor.

"You think he's dead?" whispered Hanson.

"God, I hope so..." Walton whispered back.

Lai Anh stepped forward from the trees behind them. "You're okay!" she shouted, limping forward and throwing her arms around Hanson. "When you fell I assumed that you were..."

Hanson took her under one arm and squeezed back. "It's okay. It's okay. I'd have assumed the same."

Lai Anh squealed and ducked her head as the airy scream they had heard a few minutes ago turned into a dragon like roar and two jet fighters rushed past over head, whipping the red smoke from the opposite shore into a frenzy. The Vietnam Black noticed them, throwing its head up and baring its mandibles in a display of territoriality and aggression. The surviving Viet Cong dropped their weapons and ran for the cover of the trees.

The two F-105 Thunderchiefs that had just flown past banked hard and to the left, sending a confirmation signal across the radios that the target was confirmed as red smoke. They had seen Viet Cong on the beach, and fire support was needed.

Five seconds later, Hanson, Walton and Lai Anh heard another airy scream, slightly lower in register this time. The Vietnam Black noticed it too, and ignored the small arms fire from the other Viet Cong, just for a moment, swinging its head this way and that, trying to get a sense of where the strange noise was coming from.

An F-4 Phantom came in low, skimming just above where the red smoke was dissipating, and let go its payload of BLU-1: a napalm bomb.

Hanson watched as the Phantoms pulled up hard, away from the devastating force the bomb would create. To him it seemed as though time slowed down, the finned bombs tilting on their axes and then dropping down out of the sky. Below them, covered in blood and mud, yet still somehow glistening and oddly beautiful, the Vietnam Black arced its head up to meet them, mandibles open ready to greet whatever this odd new threat might be.

The bomb struck the ground several feet behind the Vietnam Black, and to Hanson it seemed that there was a momentary pause before the black and orange fire of the Napalm billowed towards them. The fire rolled forward, blasting into the centipede, and he saw its body break under the immense force and heat of the explosion.

The napalm caught everywhere it struck: trees, mud - even the river itself catching and burning.

As one, Hanson, Walton and Lai Anh watched the centipede writhing and thrashing in the fire; a hyper aggressive ball of hate, even as it burned. It smashed its mandibles together, running in a circle, and Hanson could only imagine the hellacious noise that it must be making.

A second Phantom swooped in after the first, another wall of fire shooting across the riverside, this time obscuring the beast from view. They raised their hands to cover themselves from the heat, light and force of the explosions.

"Man, I almost thought it was going to survive," whispered Walton.

"Me too," Lai Anh replied. "They used to say that nothing could stop the Việt Nam Đen. They said that it was the heart of the jungle. When the cloud covers the moon, where even the insects fall silent, in that darkness, the night itself would give birth to the Việt Nam Đen. I never thought anything could destroy one."

"He ain't going nowhere," said Walton, pulling a fresh cigarette packet from his packet, and lighting one.

Hanson's jaw fell open. "Motherfucker, were you holding out on me?"

"Hey, I didn't know how long we'd be out here. Figured in a day or two we could use this little 'discovery'. You want one?"

"Fuck yes, I want one," interrupted Lai Anh. The two men laughed.

Hanson accepted a cigarette gratefully, and looked up into the sky. He could just about hear the rhythmic thudding of the helicopters coming in to collect them.

He wasn't sure what sort of report he could possibly give. If he told the top brass the truth - that a highly trained squad of US troops had been wiped out by a giant centipede, then the best case scenario was that they gave him a Section Eight and shipped him off to a mental hospital in Saigon for the remainder of the war. The three of them would need their stories straight.

"What are we going to tell them?"

Walton chuckled, "You mean about the bug? Yeah, the flyboys didn't seem to notice it, and if they did, then they'll never say anything about it. They're too smart for that."

"Why can't we tell them?" asked Lai Anh.

"They'll never believe us, Lai Anh," explained Hanson. "We need to just say that we were attacked by Viet Cong while investigating Hai Trang. We lost everyone else and then made our way back as best we could."

"But..."

"We can't mention the Việt Nam Đen, Lai Anh. Don't you get it? They'll think we're lying. It barely makes sense to us, so there's absolutely no way that the military will swallow it. We need to be in total agreement. As soon as those choppers land, we can't mention the Vietnam Black ever again. I'm serious about this."

"I...I understand."

Hanson turned to the gunner. "Walton, are you on board?"

The big man hesitated, then nodded. "Yeah. Yeah, you're right. To my grave, man."

The choppers came closer, and Hanson felt his relief grow.

It was over.

PART FOUR

FORTUNATE SON

CHAPTER TWENTY-ONE

In his dream, he had been back at home, working in the backyard with his grandpa. It had been a broiling hot day, and they'd both been digging a hole. He couldn't remember why they had been digging it, but it had made sense in the dream. To plant something large, or so it seemed, for the hole was at least six feet long and four feet wide. He had been about to ask his grandpa what they needed to do next when he had woken up; or at least he thought he had.

He rose to consciousness slowly and grunted a little, his throat aching and raw with thirst. In his half-awake state, he mumbled for his grandpa, even knowing then that his grandpa had only been in the dream, and was many miles from him now. He opened his eyes, and thought at first that he had the sheets wrapped over his head.

He took a deep breath and the air was so humid he felt that he was drinking it rather than breathing it. It felt heavy and warm in his lungs, and there was an earthy, dirty taste to the air, with a faint ammonia tang. He groaned in pain again. When he had breathed in it felt as though he had cracked several ribs. The stabbing ache was immediately arresting, making him wish he didn't have to breathe at all.

"Is anyone there?" he called out, his voice barely a whisper.

He'd been running, hadn't he? They'd searched the village. They'd found the tunnel and he'd gone inside with someone else. There had been a large room, like a barracks of some kind.

He coughed, sobbing at the pain in his ribs. A gentle rattle came from somewhere in the darkness. It sounded like gravel and stones tumbling lightly.

The other guy he'd come down here with had to be here somewhere. There's no way that they'd have just left him here. They liked him. They'd called him...what had they called him...

"Grandpa..." he whispered in the darkness. The rattle came again.

He was lying down. He must have fallen in the darkness, hit his head, cracked some ribs and been knocked unconscious. Yes, that's what must have happened. The rest of the squad must be looking for him by now. They'd be along any moment.

He wondered how long he'd been out for. He'd been knocked out twice previously, once during a boxing match at basic training...he'd been out for about a minute, apparently, but it had seemed instantaneous. If they hadn't have told him, he'd never have known. Another time when he was a kid, he'd banged his head on the cupboard door and been knocked out for about fifteen minutes, only waking in the car on the way to the hospital, his panicked mother holding a dishcloth to his bleeding head. Again, it had seemed instantaneous. If, in the darkness of slumber, there was no difference between sixty seconds and fifteen minutes, then who knows how long he could have been asleep down here.

Here.

Viet Cong Tunnels.

Shit. That rattle could be Charlie.

He propped himself up on his elbows, feeling his head ache painfully. Yeah, definitely a concussion.

Falconer reached down for his side arm, and felt something skitter away in the darkness. He flinched away violently. A rat, probably. Maybe a snake.

No, there had been something else down here. Something in the dark. Something big.

He reached for his holster again, found his M1911, popped the webbing strap, and drew it. He pulled back the slide to cock it, and strained to hear any noise in the darkness.

Now, he heard a strange rustling sound, and close.

He wished that there was even just a chink of light coming in here. The blackness was all consuming, and impenetrable.

That strange rustling whisper came again, and it sounded even closer than before.

It was no good, he couldn't afford to wait for rescue any longer - especially as for all he knew it had been days since he had fallen. He held the gun in his right hand, and reached out with his left to push himself upright, bracing himself for the pain in his crushed ribs.

His legs didn't work.

It wasn't that there was pain. It was just that there was no sensation and, worse, no response. Maybe he'd been laying in a strange position and they had both gone to sleep.

A chill ran through him. Maybe he'd fallen worse than he'd first thought and damaged his spine. That couldn't be possible, could it? Of course, he thought it unlikely that he could crush all his ribs like this in a fall.

Unless it wasn't a fall.

He'd been running from something.

Something in the blackness.

After a minute or two of waiting for his legs to wake up and give him sensation and mobility, he reached out with his left hand again, and this time his palm came to rest on something hard and tubular. He lifted it up, trying to see it in the pitch darkness. One end of the tube was rough, like sandpaper.

A flare.

Yes, when he'd been running, he'd dropped one. It must have fallen or rolled back to...to wherever this was.

He set his handgun on his stomach for a moment, wincing as he felt the weight of it in his lower ribs, and popped the flare, striking the ignition end against the sandpaper like cap, and held it up high.

Then the screaming began.

His entire body from waist down was covered in centipedes. They looked like the ones that the big guy - Dalton? - had picked off his back a few days ago, but these were pitch black from their antenna down to the ends of all their legs. They were all larger, too, easily ten inches long each. They writhed and ambled across his body, feeding as they went. He saw several with their heads completely sunk in his flesh. One reared up, chewing a lump of meat pulled from his thigh. He could see patches of his camouflaged pants showing through here and there, and the way they moved told him that there had to be more of the creatures that he couldn't see, feasting on his legs down to the bone.

He screamed again, batting at the ones on his crotch with his right hand, holding the flare aloft in the other. Two were sent flying, but two more flashed up and clamped down with their wicked, barbed mandibles. He shook his hand viciously, but they bit harder, one slicing completely through the flesh on the edge of his palm and falling to the ground, scurrying into the darkness.

He heard another sound, this time like concrete slabs sliding in the darkness, and he waved the flare around desperately, eyes wide open.

He saw something large moving in the darkness. In a flash it all came back to him. The thing he had been running from. All black, blades, pure aggression and hate. A snake from hell. A centipede from the deepest darkness of the earth.

This one didn't seem quite the same, though. In the white neon glare of the flare, it had a reddish tint, a blood red colour. He saw the antenna wave, heard the clicking of mandibles...

God, this one was larger than the last...

The Vietnam Red studied him for a moment, her red, shining eyes squinting evilly. After studying him for a second, she turned away, and lay back down in a slumber, with a rasping sigh.

Falconer watched her in the darkness until the signal flare sputtered and died.

After a minute or so, he reached down to the M1911, hoping he had at least one bullet left.

Then, he lay in the darkness, listening to the sound of the bugs feasting on his legs, genitals and stomach, and thought about his mother, and hoped that she'd be okay. Then he dreamed a little of coming home, a little of Audrey, and again of his grandpa digging that hole in the dirt.

THE END

ABOUT THE AUTHOR

Brad Harmer-Barnes is a British horror author who grew up watching 1950s "creature feature" movies and 1980s action and slasher movies, as well as reading H.P. Lovecraft, M.R. James, Stephen King, Brian Lumley and Clive Barker. Outside of writing, he enjoys tabletop gaming, collecting obscure soundtracks on vinyl, and trying to get through as much of his "To Read" pile as possible. His other books, *North Sea Hunters*, a tale of giant shark versus submarine, and *Tempest* Outpost, a tale of brain-controlling Lovecraftian spiders, are also available from Severed Press.

You can follow him on Twitter and Instagram @realbradhb, and he is also a regular guest on comedy podcast *The Crazy Train*.

CHECK OUT OTHER GREAT HORROR NOVELS

MONSTROSITY
by Tim Curran

The Food. It seeped from the ground, a living, gushing, teratogenic nightmare. It contaminated anything that ate it, causing nature to run wild with horrible mutations, creating massive monstrosities that roam the land destroying towns and cities, feeding on livestock and human beings and one another. Now Frank Bowman, an ordinary farmer with no military skills, must get his children to safety. And that will mean a trip through the contaminated zone of monsters, madmen, and The Food itself. Only a fool would attempt it. Or a man with a mission.

THE SQUIRMING
by Jack Hamlyn

You are their hosts

You are their food.

The parasites came out of nowhere, squirming horrors that enslaved the human race. They turned the population into mindless pack animals, psychotic cannibalistic hordes whose only purpose was to feed them.

Now with the human race teetering at the edge of extinction, extermination teams are fighting back, killing off the parasites and their voracious hosts. Taking them out one by one in violent, bloody encounters.

The future of mankind is at stake.

And time is running out.

CHECK OUT OTHER GREAT HORROR NOVELS

DEATH CRAWLERS
by Gerry Griffiths

Worldwide, there are thought to be 8,000 species of centipede, of which, only 3,000 have been scientifically recorded. The venom of Scolopendra gigantea—the largest of the arthropod genus found in the Amazon rainforest—is so potent that it is fatal to small animals and toxic to humans. But when a cargo plane departs the Amazon region and crashes inside a national park in the United States, much larger and deadlier creatures escape the wreckage to roam wild, reproducing at an astounding rate. Entomologist, Frank Travis solicits small town sheriff Wanda Rafferty's help and together they investigate the crash site. But as a rash of gruesome deaths befalls the townsfolk of Prospect, Frank and Wanda will soon discover how vicious and cunning these new breed of predators can be. Meanwhile, Jake and Nora Carver, and another backpacking couple, are venturing up into the mountainous terrain of the park. If only they knew their fun-filled weekend is about to become a living nightmare.

THE PULLER
by Michael Hodges

Matt Kearns has two choices: fight or hide. The creature in the orchard took the rest. Three days ago, he arrived at his favorite place in the world, a remote shack in Michigan's Upper Peninsula. The plan was to mourn his father's death and figure out his life. Now he's fighting for it. An invisible creature has him trapped. Every time Matt tries to flee, he's dragged backwards by an unseen force. Alone and with no hope of rescue, Matt must escape the Puller's reach. But how do you free yourself from something you cannot see?

CHECK OUT OTHER GREAT HORROR NOVELS

BLACK FRIDAY
by Michael Hodges

Jared the kleptomaniac, Chike the unemployed IT guy, Patricia the shopaholic, and Jeff the meth dealer are trapped inside a Chicago supermall on Black Friday. Bridgefield Mall empties during a fire alarm, and most of the shoppers drive off into a strange mist surrounding the mall parking lot. They never return. Chike and his group try calling friends and family, but their smart phones won't work, not even Twitter. As the mist creeps closer, the mall lights flicker and surge. Bulbs shatter and spray glass into the air. Unsettling noises are heard from within the mist, as the meth dealer becomes unhinged and hunts the group within the mall. Cornered by the mist, and hunted from within, Chike and the survivors must fight for their lives while solving the mystery of what happened to Bridgefield Mall. Sometimes, a good sale just isn't worth it.

GRIMWEAVE
by Tim Curran

In the deepest, darkest jungles of Indochina, an ancient evil is waiting in a forgotten, primeval valley. It is patient, monstrous, and bloodthirsty. Perfectly adapted to its hot, steaming environment, it strikes silent and stealthy, it chosen prey: human. Now Michael Spiers, a Marine sniper, the only survivor of a previous encounter with the beast, is going after it again. Against his better judgement, he is made part of a Marine Force Recon team that will hunt it down and destroy it.

The hunters are about to become the hunted.